TRAP

DARK MASQUE BOOK 3

MAGGIE ALABASTER

JO BRADLEY

Cover by Moonstruck Cover Design and Photography

Edited by Lily Luchesi

Proofread by Nora Hogan

CHAPTER ONE

KENNEDY

The darkness was unrelenting.

Eyes open.

Eyes closed.

It made no difference. There was nothing here but me and the endless ringing in my ears.

I found a bucket in the corner I could use for a toilet, but what I really needed was a drink of water. Food too, but mostly water.

After a few hours, I started to talk to myself. Softly at first, just to hear a sound. Then I sang for a while before my throat got too dry and I had to stop.

I began to wish I was chained to the ceiling in Ice's workshop, having him peel off layers of skin. He gave his victims water, and a break from the torture.

This... This was unrelenting. I had no idea if it was days or hours. Time had no meaning here.

If there was a positive side, it was that I had a lot of time to think. I had no shortage of thoughts and questions that had no answers. They started with— was Ice in a room like this? Was he still alive? Was he being tortured like he tortured Frank Nixon and fuck knows how many others?

Those thoughts lead to wondering where Mannix and Ares were. We became separated when Bell's men blew up our car. Ice threw himself over me to keep me safe. I had no idea where the other guys went or if they were still alive. They might be dead, or they might be in the room next door.

I thought about shouting for them, but they wouldn't hear me. The whole point of this room was that *no one* could hear me, and I couldn't hear them. I could shout myself hoarse and it wouldn't get me anywhere. Nowhere other than thirstier than I already was. My mouth was so dry, I felt like I'd swallowed a desert.

The other thought I kept coming back to was regret. If I hadn't reactivated the virus on Bell's computer, I'd be dead right now. The only reason I was still alive and in here was because I pissed him off. I'd be dead soon enough. He wanted to make me suffer first.

Congratulations, I thought, *mission accomplished*. This was the most fucked up piece of misery I'd ever had the misfortune to experience.

For the first couple of hours, I was in denial that I was stuck here for any length of time. Then came anger.

Honestly, if anyone opened the door, I'd be happy to move on to the bargaining stage. I wasn't sure if there was anything I wouldn't do to get the hell out of here.

The door remained firmly closed.

I began to fixate on how they made a door that had absolutely no gaps. Maybe it had gaps, but the corridor outside was too dark to show them. The corridor might be a similar bottomless pit of sensory deprivation. I barely remember being brought down it.

Great, now my memory was fucked up. Was I concussed after the explosion? I felt around my head, but found no lumps or bumps or blood.

I curled up in a corner and tried to sleep. Why a corner, I don't know. I guess it felt safer than sleeping in the middle of the room. There was some logic behind it, but where I slept was unlikely to make any difference if someone came for me.

Whatever, it made me feel better for a minute or two.

I got a non-zero amount of sleep, but hell if I know how long it was. When I awoke, I was surprised I was still alive.

I was disappointed too. Disappointed to wake up still here. Disappointed to wake up at all.

Fuck my life.

If I could do it all over, would I do it the same way?

I had no answer for that question. Bell tried to have me killed. Having his computer systems scrambled and screwed up was small in comparison to that.

On the other hand, I could have let the grudge go and moved on with my life, knowing he'd come after me again at some point. It wasn't even about me at the time. Samuel Bell wanted to get at my stepfather, Leo Cassani. He decided to go via me. Kennedy Knight, computer science student and owner of a gymnastics studio.

I was nothing in the scheme of things, but he came after me anyway.

And me, well, apparently I hold a grudge.

Since I was never walking back out of Bell's

house alive, I'd decided I might as well take his systems down with me.

I could have restored most of what the virus impacted. All he'd needed to do was assure me I'd leave in one piece. And Ice along with me. A promise not to try again later to kill me wouldn't go astray either.

Would I have believed him if he gave me such an assurance? Probably not, but I might not have ended up here. At best, I would have spent the rest of my days looking over my shoulder, just in case.

Yeah, that didn't sound like much of a life to me, either. It would have been a fuck ton better than this.

I breathed a mouthful of dry air into my parched throat. I should try to do some stretching exercises to keep myself limber and sane, but I also needed to save my strength and what little moisture I had left.

Sanity wouldn't be any use to me if I was dead.

I pushed myself to my feet and decided on some gentle stretching.

Curious, I raised a hand above me. I couldn't touch the ceiling. One mistake whoever built this room made, thank fuck, was the ceiling height.

If they wanted to torture someone even more than depriving them of sight and sound, they'd make the ceiling too low to stand, and the walls too close together to lie down.

Ice would get a laugh out of that thought. He got a laugh out of a lot of strange and twisted things. Mannix said he was fucked in the head. Maybe he was. I thought he was just a bit different, that was all. Just a bit weird. There was nothing wrong with being weird.

Shit. My thoughts were getting more scattered and random.

I raised my hands in front of me and walked the handful of steps to the opposite wall.

I grazed my hands on the stone and wondered what it would take to smash my way out.

Since this room was underground, it was unlikely there'd be anywhere to go. Since I had nothing to smash it with, this whole line of thought was moot. I had a moment of cheer imagining bringing the whole house down on top of me and everyone in it.

Sadistic? Maybe.

Satisfying as hell? Definitely.

I turned around and walked a few steps back the other way until I reached the door.

I ran my fingers up and down in case there was a weakness I hadn't felt before. If there was, I didn't find it now either. There wasn't even a knob or a handle, or a keyhole to pick through.

Nothing but a solid, metal door, probably as thick as my arm. I rapped my knuckles on it in a mixture of curiosity, frustration and the need to hear some sound.

It wasn't hollow and didn't even give slightly. Whoever put this door here meant for it to stay for a long, long time.

"Sadistic asshole," I muttered. Who put a torture chamber in a multimillion dollar harbourfront mansion?

Yeah, there could be a lot more of them than anyone knows about. I remembered one of the guys telling me how a house down the street sank into a sinkhole a while ago. Maybe it wasn't a sinkhole, or a random occurrence. Maybe it was a room like this, collapsing in on itself. How long had it been there? It might predate the house. If another, similar room collapsed, then so could this.

I waited, but nothing happened. Not even a rumble of the earth shifting, or the walls caving in.

I wanted to pound on the door and insist they let me out, or at least feed me and give me something to drink. That would be a waste of time and strength. If the door was as thick as it seemed, no one was going to hear me. I could scream at the top of my lungs and no one would ever know. There might be someone a metre or two away from me doing just that.

If the space was bigger, it would be the perfect place for a loud party. We could turn the music up full volume and not bother the neighbours.

There my thoughts went again, being scattered and random. How long would it be before I started to giggle to myself or something like that?

What is it they say? No one knows how to shred a human better than another human. People spent thousands of years perfecting torture methods and ways of fucking with each other. Hell, I learnt about a few of them at uni when I studied psychology. Ares probably knew a bunch more. Ice too.

I leaned my forehead on the cool of the door, and tried not to let tears get the better of me. If I had the tears to cry, I didn't have them to spare.

Focus on being angry, I told myself. *Crying won't get you anywhere.* I could hold anger as well as I held a grudge, but if I cried, then Samuel Bell won. If I slammed my fists into the door over and over until they were a bloody mess, he won.

Guess what happened if I completely lost my mind, or died in the corner of dehydration.

Yeah, he won.

Fuck that.

I lifted my head and placed my palms on the door. Under my fingertips were barely noticeable dents in the metal. I felt around them and decided they were indentations from fists. I bet if I felt down lower, I'd find indentations from feet, or shoes.

"You don't get to win, asshole," I said to the darkness. I didn't shout. My voice was barely above a whisper, but the words sounded loud in my ears. Hoarse and forced.

"You don't get to win," I said again. "I might die here, but I'm not giving up until the last breath leaves my body. I'm not going to cry or go insane. I'm not going to try to break down the door or the walls. I'm going to conserve as much of my strength as possible. At some point, someone is going to come and check on me, and I'll still be alive. You know how I know that? Because there's no bones down here. You don't shove people in here and let them die. There's no smell of death, no hint that anyone has ever actually died in here."

I might be clutching at straws. A hundred people could have died in here and Bell's people were that good at cleaning up.

I pushed the thought away. I liked my theory

better. It was much better for my mental health to think people got out of here in one piece.

Any moment, someone would come and open the door. They might even apologise for keeping me down here for so long. They misunderstood. They were supposed to take me to some fancy guest room while I thought about what I did. They'd bring me a tray of bacon, eggs and toast, along with a soup cup-sized coffee.

I leaned my head back against the door and exhaled. I was losing it. He might just win after all.

The door still stayed firmly closed.

CHAPTER TWO

KENNEDY

Click.

Something jolted me awake.

I shot up. What the—

I pressed my back and the palms of my hands against the wall. Blinked, in case I was hallucinating.

The difference was subtle, but the darkness wasn't absolute anymore. It took me a moment to realise the door was opening. The corridor outside was dimly lit, but the difference was almost night and day.

I pushed myself up the wall and stood pressed against it.

"Who's there?"

The response was an almost blinding light right in my eyes.

I threw my hand up in front of my face and winced.

"My father wants to see you." Female voice, about my age.

She lowered the phone.

I lowered my hand.

She wasn't Lila. It wasn't difficult to guess who she was.

Chloe Bell shared the same sharp edge and cold eyes as her sister and father.

She wasn't identical to her twin sister, but the resemblance was strong. They both had dark hair and heart shaped faces. Chloe's lips were fuller, and she was slightly taller.

"Unless you want to stay here, I suggest you come with me." She had no gun that I could see, but her tone suggested she expected me to obey.

I would, because pretty much anything would be better than being locked down here.

My eyes on her, watching for any movement, any sign she might come at me, I stepped through the door and into the corridor.

"You stink." She wrinkled her nose.

"Someone forgot to install a shower in there," I said dryly.

She looked at me for a moment, then laughed.

"Yeah, I guess they did. I think that shithole predates plumbing." She didn't seem to approve of her father locking people in there.

What do you know? We had that in common.

"Where's Ice?" She seemed more reasonable than her sister, but that might be a good cop, bad cop act. A ruse to get me to trust her. The joke was on her if she thought that would happen. I wasn't that naive anymore.

"If I had to guess, Dad is keeping him locked away somewhere to ensure your behaviour." She shrugged one shoulder and tapped on the door at the end of the corridor.

The door was opened from the other side. She stepped through and gestured for me to do the same.

I eyed the guard as I walked past, but she looked back at me, unblinking.

"Why does he care if I behave?" I asked. "Isn't he going to kill me?"

"If he wanted you dead, you'd be dead," she said bluntly. After a moment she spoke again. "I don't know what he wants you for."

If it was worse than death or sensory deprivation, then it would probably suck. Or he thought I would.

I wasn't sure what I'd do if that was what he expected in return for letting me live. Becoming a sex slave for someone like him wasn't on my list of career choices. Would I have a choice? The alternative might not be death, it might be going back to that room.

I wasn't prepared for the surge of fear and desperation at the thought of that. I couldn't go back there. I'd rather be covered in honey and tied to an anthill than go back there.

I was about to ask for a drink of water when I realised she was leading me into a huge, opulent kitchen. It was a study in white, veined marble, and rich, hardwood floors. Past the kitchen was a sitting area with a stunning view of the harbour. The view alone was worth millions.

She reached into an upper cabinet and pulled out a glass. She handed it to me and stood back.

"No doubt you're thirsty." She waved towards the gooseneck tap that arched over a massive farmhouse style sink. She watched me carefully, clearly mindful that I could break the glass and use it as a weapon.

Instead, I stepped over to the sink and filled the glass to the top. I gulped it down and refilled the glass. I drank the second one more slowly. If I drank too fast, I'd throw it all back up. That would be a waste of precious moisture.

It tasted better than chocolate.

After a third glass of water, I set the empty glass on the benchtop beside the sink and nodded my thanks.

"Is this something you have to do often?" It was much easier to talk now with a lubricated throat.

"Not now that I'm usually away at school," she said. She glanced at her phone. "I'll take you to my father's study, then I have to catch the train back to Brutham."

I remembered what the guys said about Brutham Academy. How the third and fourth year students got to hunt the first years, and how a lot of the first years didn't make it out alive. They said the twins, Hunter and Parker, would help Lila. I wondered who would help Chloe. In spite of her last name, she seemed nicer than any Bell I met so far.

"I don't suppose there's any chance I could go with you instead of going to his study?" I asked hopefully. "I quite enjoy train travel." Especially if I ended up a long way from here.

Her regret almost seemed sincere, but it was as firm as the locked door was. "You wouldn't get past the front door."

I sighed. "I had a feeling you'd say something like that." We passed a few guards on the way. They all watched both of us like hawks, especially me. I thought about making a run for it, but I'd be lucky to make it more than five or six steps.

She nodded and led me back toward the office where all of this started in the first place. She knocked on the door and waited a moment before she opened it and went inside.

Regretting my life choices, I followed.

Samuel Bell was behind his desk, unpacking what looked like a brand-new computer. State-of-the-art, top-of-the-line, memory for days. I couldn't help being a little envious. I had a decent laptop, but it was nothing compared to this. Of course, the right person could build a better computer, but it was impressive nonetheless.

He paused in his unboxing and scowled at me. His gaze slipped from me to Chloe and he nodded.

Without another word, she slipped back out the door and closed it behind her.

He went back to unpacking while I stood near the door waiting, and watching. The message was clear. When he was ready, he'd speak to me. Fine, whatever. There was sunshine coming through the window behind him. I could stand here for as long as it took, enjoying the fact it wasn't darkness.

Finally, he looked back up. "As you see, I needed a new computer. The other one was...compromised."

Yeah, that was a nice way of saying it was fucked.

He continued. "Fortunately, it wasn't connected to my wider network. Just a smaller one within the house. Replacing all my files will take some time, but no more than three or four hours. What you did, it caused a minor inconvenience."

Well that sucked. I was locked in that room for how long, over a minor inconvenience? He was a vindictive asshole, wasn't he?

"However," he pulled a keyboard out of its packaging, "I needed a new computer anyway. This gave me the excuse to get around to buying one."

So I did him a favour. What did I get in return for that? A medal? My own private island? My freedom?

"I'm impressed with your computer skills. None of the people I currently have working for me could have done what you did as quickly as you did. None of them would have had the balls to sneak into my office during a party to do it either."

How did I respond to that?

"I like a challenge." I wasn't sure if that was the right response, but that was what came out of my mouth.

"So it would seem." He tossed the packaging aside and placed the keyboard in front of the screen.

I stared at him. Was that all he could say?

"Am I here to set that up for you?" I nodded toward the computer. "Because you didn't need to lock me away for that."

He chuckled. "It's good to see a stay in the basement didn't break you. I didn't think it would. No one who did what you and those three boys did would break that easily."

"I'll be sure to add that to my badass card application form," I said sarcastically. I should have the required amount of points by now, right?

He surprised me by saying, "I want you to work for me." Before I could respond, he raised a hand. "We both know that's not going to happen. Leo Cassani would never allow his stepdaughter to work for the enemy. Neither would his son. I hear they keep you on a short leash."

I couldn't keep the annoyance of my face. "I'm not on a—" I cut myself off. He was trying to get a rise out of me and it wouldn't work. "What do you *really* want?"

He stepped around to the other side of his desk and leaned against it, his arms crossed. He gazed at me with dark brown eyes that seemed to bore right into my soul.

Up close, I saw he hadn't shaved for a couple of

days. Dressed in a dark suit, perfectly tailored, an expensive watch and shoes I could have seen my reflection in, he looked like a rich mobster.

I reminded myself that he was exactly what he was, and returned his gaze.

"You're not scared of me." It was a statement, not a question.

I was terrified, but trying not to show it. It was nice to know I succeeded in something at least. I failed in messing up his computer system, and apparently he wasn't bothered that he tried to kill me.

I resisted the urge to lick my lips. "Should I be? The worst you can do is kill me." Or put me back in the basement.

His lips twisted up in a smile that gave me the shivers. "You should be very scared of me." His voice was low, almost pleasant except the knot of threat tied around it.

"There's nothing I can't do to you or *with* you. No one to help you. No one to stop me. And when I'm done with you, I could make you disappear so thoroughly no one will know you ever existed."

His words sent a pulse of fear right through me. He was right, he could do all of that and more.

"But you're not going to," I said slowly. This wasn't about sex or torture, there was something else going on here. I didn't have the foggiest idea what it was. I wasn't sure I wanted to know. The only thing I was sure of, he wouldn't give me a choice.

"I'm not?" He seemed amused.

"No, you're not. Because you need me for something." A man like him would have women falling over themselves to sleep with him, and enough money to pay his minions to do whatever he wanted. No, there was something else going on here. He needed something from me no one else could give.

"Smart girl," he said approvingly. "As it happens, I do need something."

CHAPTER THREE

KENNEDY

"Hey," I greeted Ice more cheerfully than I felt.

Too many thoughts battled with each other in my brain. Could I do what Bell wanted me to do? Did I want to? The implications of everything he said to me hadn't even started to sink in. How long would it take until they did?

Those were questions and answers for another day. Right now I wanted to get out of here. Preferably before Bell changed his mind. A man like him could and would do exactly that, just because he was able to. He'd find a way to get what he wanted done with or without my help.

"Finally. I was getting bored." Ice was chained to the wall with his hands above his head. The chain was so short, the bolt so high up, he stood on his toes.

"That looks painful." How was he not screaming? I wanted to scream just looking at him.

He glanced down. "Yeah, it's a bit tedious. As torture methods go, it's simple but effective. Not as effective as the boredom. A guy like me needs mental stimulation."

"They could have put on the TV and put on something you hate," I pointed out. I didn't know what that was. I wasn't in a position to trash talk anyone's TV choices, since I watched a lot of different things. Some things were better than others.

"Like cricket?" He grimaced. "Yeah, that would have been much worse. How are things with you? It's good to see you're still alive and hot as ever." He looked me up and down.

Leave it to Ice to flirt with me while hanging from the ceiling.

"I could use a shower, but I'm here to get you out of here. We should hurry, I think that guard overheard what you said about cricket." We might both end up chained to the ceiling with the sport on some big-screen we couldn't ignore.

That would still be better than the basement.

"We get to go home?" He cocked his head at me in question. Then his eyes turned to steel. "What did

you have to do to get us out of here? If he touched
you—"

"He didn't," I said quickly. "We didn't do as much
damage as we hoped to do, so he's letting us go." That
was the truth, but not all of it. I'd tell him everything
later, when we were out of here. I couldn't guarantee
what might happen otherwise.

I stepped aside as a guard with a key unlocked
Ice's chains.

The guard also stepped aside, letting Ice fall hard
to the concrete floor on his knees.

He grunted in pain. "I might have overestimated
how much weight my feet could take after standing
on tiptoe for hours." He rubbed his wrists and
managed to clamber to his feet before I could move
to help him.

"Are you okay?" I couldn't carry him, and I
doubted Bell would offer any help. I could really use
Mannix and Ares right now. I wished I knew what
happened to them. If they were dead...

I couldn't let myself think that. I had to focus on
getting Ice and me out of here.

"It takes more than a little chain to slow down the
Iceman." He smiled, but it was forced. His feet and
wrists clearly hurt more than he was willing to show.
He was as stubborn as me. And, for now, as alive.

In spite of that, he let me put an arm around him before we walked out the corridor.

All this time, he was in the room next to me. He'd had light from the bulb in the ceiling. And water, judging by a jug on the table in the corner.

Evidently Bell liked some variety in his torture. Fair enough, so did Ice.

The first few minutes were slow going, especially the slog up the steps into the back of the house. Ice tried not to let on that he was in pain, but I saw it in his eyes and in the way he gingerly stepped from tread to tread.

"Lucky they're not too inventive here," he whispered. "I would have broken my toes and *then* strung me up like that."

"I don't think you should give them any ideas," I whispered back. "They might do that next time."

"Let's hope there isn't next time." He fell silent then, focusing on his breathing and putting one foot in front of the other.

The guards led us out the door and around to the gate. Neither of them looked impressed having to open it and usher us out. They both kept their hands near guns on their hips, their eyes on us.

They clearly wondered why the hell Bell was letting us go.

I could imagine the speculation in their minds. Mostly involving me bent over or on my knees. If only they knew the real reason. Everyone would know soon enough.

I flashed them both a smile as we stepped out onto the street. My heart was racing. Palms coated with sweat. I waited, but neither guard drew their weapon.

They stepped back through the gate and closed it behind them.

"How about that," Ice said. "They're actually letting us go. I thought they were going to shoot us and leave us on the street as a warning to anyone going past." He turned around and looked up at the fence. "Those spikes would be perfect for the heads of their enemies to languish on."

"That might have been acceptable practice back in the dark ages, but it wouldn't go unnoticed in the middle of Sydney," I said wryly.

Although, it was unlikely anyone walking past would think they were real. They'd assume they were something to do with Halloween or April Fools' Day, or whatever. They'd probably take photos and talk about how realistic they looked and how they rotted realistically as the days passed. The fucking videos would probably go viral.

"That's true." Ice almost seemed sad about the fact. "We could do it in Dusk Bay. Leo's house is remote enough to have a couple of heads on the gate for a few days." He actually seemed to consider the idea.

"I don't think Leo would appreciate having heads on his fence. I know my mother wouldn't like the idea." At least, I didn't *think* she would. Who even knew at this point? Right now I wasn't sure if the sky was actually blue. If I had a rug under my feet, it was gone now.

Ice pouted playfully but quickly seemed to forget about the idea. "They've cleaned up where the car exploded." He nodded in that direction.

I followed his gaze. Whoever cleaned up did an amazing job. There was almost no sign of any fire or explosion. There was a faint singe mark on the road, but no shattered glass, nothing. There weren't even any bloodstains on the road. No indication the authorities were here. It was as though the whole thing hadn't happened at all.

If I wasn't there, trying not to be blown up or shot, I wouldn't have believed it. We stood on just another quiet street in an affluent part of Sydney.

"We need to find out what happened to Mannix and Ares," I said. "Do you think they..."

"Found somewhere safe to stash themselves until this blew over? Definitely." He nodded. "In fact, I know exactly where they would have gone." He ran a hand over the back of his head and straightened his messy bun.

"Need a lift?" I didn't even see one of the twins until they stepped out of the dark SUV parked a few cars down. "Hunter and I are waiting for Lila, but if it's the place I'm thinking of, it's not far."

I hadn't noticed before that Parker had a slightly crooked nose. From the look of it, someone broke it for him. Whoever they were, they were my hero. I'd happily give Hunter a matching nose with a baseball bat. Or a chair. Or a brick. I wasn't fussy.

"Why the fuck should we go anywhere with you?" I said at the same time as Ice said, "Sure."

We exchanged looks.

"You trust them?" I asked, unable to believe he'd consider getting in a car with those assholes.

"Fuck no, but right now we need a ride, and they're offering. Unless you feel like an hour walk, then they're our best bet. Besides, they wouldn't betray us twice, unless they really hate living. Because the minute Bell finds out they're out here waiting for his daughter who they're not supposed to be anywhere near, he's going to kill them." Ice gave them a pointed look and opened his mouth like he might shout loud enough for Bell to hear.

"Your boyfriend makes a compelling case," Parker said quickly. "Hop in."

Without waiting for a response, he slipped back into the car and closed the door behind him.

No wonder I hadn't noticed them before, the windows were heavily tinted. I guess it's something you do if you're lurking around outside your girlfriend's house when her father potentially wants you dead.

I couldn't decide if they were that dumb or had balls for sticking around where they clearly weren't wanted. A combination of the two, perhaps. Love made people do some pretty strange things, including lurking and risking death.

"This is crazy." I stepped over to the back of the car, but stopped with my hand on the handle.

"You say that like crazy is a bad thing." Ice grinned. He put his hand over mine and opened the car door. As if to prove it was safe, he climbed inside first.

I sighed, shook my head and followed him in. He was right, an hour walk would suck, especially with no shoes. Who else could the twins betray us to now anyway? Bell let us go, there was no point taking us back.

At least, I fucking hoped not.

"Hey," Hunter greeted as the door clunked closed behind me. "Good to see you alive and kicking. I thought you guys were toast."

"Fuck off," I told him. Yeah, he did have a perfectly straight nose. On one hand, it was a good way to tell them apart. On the other, it would be fun to see him suffer.

Hunter clicked his tongue. "Don't be like that. We didn't have a choice, but we're genuinely glad you're not dead. We are on the same side, after all."

I sat forward. "The only side you two are on is your own. If it benefited you, you'd kill us or drop us off with...someone."

"Of course we would," Hunter agreed. "But right now, what benefits us is you two being alive. If you weren't, we'd have had to explain to Reuben what happened. And then we'd have to tell him where we were and why. And then we'd have to face him being angry. Trust me, you don't want to see Reuben angry. He's not very nice when he's not angry. When he is..."

I leaned my arms on the back of the seat in front of me. "Am I supposed to give a shit if your brother is angry with you? Because I have news for you, I don't." Maybe it was Reuben who broke Parker's nose. Or someone who worked for him. If that was the case, maybe Reuben wasn't so bad.

"Why did Bell let you go?" Parker asked. "Let me guess, one of you can do something for him that no one else can do." The question hung in the air, so heavy it was difficult to breathe.

My only answer was to sit back and click my seatbelt into place.

In the corner of my eye, Ice watched me speculatively. I knew he knew Parker was right, but he wasn't going to ask about it in front of them. I sure as hell wasn't going to talk about it in front of them.

I didn't want to keep secrets from him, but I had no idea what he or the other guys would think when I told them.

CHAPTER FOUR

ARES

"This is bullshit." I paced back and forth, stopping every so often to peer out between the curtains. "We should have stayed."

I scowled over at Mannix, who was no way as fucking calm as he was trying to pretend he was. That was bullshit too. No one bought his façade. He might as well have spent the last twenty-four hours stalking back across the room the way I was. We could have taken turns. There wasn't enough room for two caged lions to flex their muscles and anger.

"I made the right call," he said in that tone he learned from his father. The one that says, 'Don't question me. Don't fuck with me or I'll fuck back.' The one I wasn't in the mood to listen to.

"Yeah? How long are we going to wait and hope they turn up? Another hour? A week? They could be fucking dead for all we know."

The words stung my throat as I said them. I couldn't even speak their names. They should be here with us. Ice and Kennedy. They were ours. Mine. If they were dead, I was going to start a war, even if it was me alone against everyone else.

But I wouldn't be alone. Mannix would be beside me, trying to call the shots. Trying to be a general. He was a bossy prick, but he was usually right.

That was the hardest fucking part of all of this. When the car exploded, we went one way and Kennedy and Ice went the other. I tried to follow, but a handful of Bell's minions cut us off. We barely managed to evade them. We quietly killed a couple but then we had to hide.

The next thing we knew, the place was swarming with cops and we were forced to slip away.

Mannix insisted we come here to one of his family's safe houses and wait for Ice and Kennedy to show up.

And so, we waited, catching an hour or two of sleep here and there. I wanted to go back and look for them, but Mannix was insistent.

"They're not dead." He barely even blinked. His face was carved from stone. When he spoke, his mouth barely moved. His eyes were locked on the gap in the curtains. His hands were curled around the arms of the chair he'd sat in for the last three or four hours.

"You can't know that—"

"They're not dead," he said again. "I'd know if they were." His gaze flicked over to me and, for the first time, he seemed uncertain. Not whether they were alive or not, because he clearly believed that deep in his soul. He was uncertain about what he'd do if he was wrong.

"I don't want to lose them either," I muttered, my chin close to my chest. I wasn't good at this sharing emotions stuff.

Neither was Mannix. He'd claimed both of them as his. That was about as close to saying, 'I love you,' as I'd ever seen from him.

I hadn't even done that much. Kennedy was mine, but so far I'd resisted telling her that. When I saw her next I'd let her know she belonged to me, the same as she belonged to Mannix and Ice.

I'd claim every centimetre of her. Bury my cock so deep inside her I might get lost and never find a way out. By the time I was done, she'd understand that she was my territory.

Mine and Mannix's and Ice's. If any other man ever touched her, I'd break their neck.

The side of Mannix's mouth twitched. "Told you you didn't hate her. You're a stubborn prick."

I flipped him off. "I never hated her, I just do shit in my own time." The moment I saw her, I wanted to tear her clothes off, tie her to my bed and fuck her brains out. If she was any other woman, I would have.

When we met, she seemed so innocent, so sweet, so fragile. Goes to show first impressions aren't always right, because she's fucking none of those things. Especially fragile. If anyone suggested she was stronger than me, I'd rip off their nuts and shove them up their ass, but she was.

"We need to go back to Bell's shithole." The mansion itself was nice enough. Nicer than any place I lived as a kid by a long way, but anywhere Samuel Bell, his asshole family and his asshole minions tainted everywhere they went.

We shouldn't have planted a virus in there. We should have planted a bomb. We could have taken out a bunch of them in one shot. I bet Reuben fucking Brantley would be impressed if we took out his biggest rival.

Unfortunately, anything that big wouldn't go unnoticed by the cops. Even if Brantley paid them off, they'd have to find a scapegoat and we'd be the ones thrown right under the bus.

Fuck that.

"If they're inside, we can't help them." His stony expression was back. "If they're dead, we can't help them. We can only assume they got away and will make their way here. Ice knows to come here. He'll find a way." He didn't want me to keep arguing, but I wasn't done.

I wouldn't be done until I saw them both with my own eyes.

"And if he and Kennedy got separated?" I asked. "She won't know to come here." We should have fucking told her, but we were so convinced we knew exactly what we were doing. That we'd all get out in one piece. We got cocky.

If I wanted to be an asshole, I'd suggest it was Mannix who got cocky. He was the one leading us. He was calling the shots. I could lay all the blame on him and have an excuse to punch his lights out.

But either Ice or I could have told Kennedy about this place and Mannix would have agreed that she needed to know. Hell, he would have shown her on a map on her phone and made sure she knew exactly how to get here.

If she didn't know where to go, it was the fault of all of us. If she was lost or dead, I was as much to blame as anyone.

Fuck.

Mannix pressed his lips together so hard they turned white. "If she doesn't come here, she'll go back to Dusk Bay. Or she'll contact her mother, who'll let us know. She's resourceful, and smart." He shot me a challenging look, as though I'd deny his statement.

I wouldn't. He was right on both counts. Kennedy was the smartest person I ever met.

And she had the best tits. All I wanted to do right now was run my tongue all the way over them and bite her nipples until she screamed. And then go on biting them.

"How long are we going to wait?" I asked again.

We couldn't sit here forever in the hope they turned up or we got a phone call telling us where they were. Sooner or later we have to go home to Dusk Bay and face Mannix's family. They'd want to know if we succeeded in our mission. No doubt they'd want every minute detail of it.

They had plenty of information on Samuel Bell's place, but if there was a chance we saw something no one knew about before, they'd want to know about it. Fuck only knows if we had. It wasn't like the higher ups in the organisation told guys like us much of anything. We were the worker ants, expected to do what we were told and not ask too many questions. At the same time, we were expected to risk our lives at the drop of a hat, because right now, we were expendable.

At least, unless Kennedy's virus worked the way it was supposed to. We'd be a lot less expendable with something like that on our resumés.

Before Mannix could answer, I said, "Don't say as long as it takes. Not unless you know exactly how long that will be." I didn't need any half assed promises, or vague responses. That wasn't who I was. That wasn't who Mannix was either. We got shit done.

Not today. Today we sat in a small room in Sydney, maybe ten or so kilometres from Bell's place, breath held like we might run out of oxygen at any minute.

He tipped his chin back, his gaze grazing the ceiling. "I know we can't stay here forever." He exhaled out his nose in frustration. "We'll stay until morning.

If they don't turn up, we'll go back home." Every word seemed to cause him physical pain.

I knew he wanted to tear off heads as much as I did. I also knew what the repercussions would be for him if he did. He was supposed to take over from his father someday. If he went off half-cocked, that would never happen. And because he was Mannix, he'd never go off half cocked. He'd go off full-cocked and burn the world down to find Kennedy and Ice. He'd make people pay for anything they did to them.

And me, I'd be right beside him every step of the journey. Between us, we'd leave the world in ashes and have no regrets doing it.

I nodded. That was the best I was going to get. There was no point in pushing him further.

"Get some rest," he said. "Pacing around like that isn't gonna help anyone."

"It's helping me," I snapped. In spite of that, I perched myself on the edge of one of the beds and flopped back. If I counted the stains on the ceiling, that would pass a minute or two. I could spend another couple of minutes speculating on what exactly the stains were, but I didn't particularly want to know. Probably blood and cum. How it got there was anyone's guess. I didn't give a shit.

Ice, on the other hand, he'd be fascinated. And

impressed if any guy managed to cum all the way up there. The guy was fascinated with all sorts of weird crap like that. Things no one else would notice, much less care about. He was like a kid, endlessly looking at the world around him and trying to dissect it, either literally or figuratively. Usually literally. I've never met anyone who liked to slice things up as much as he did.

In some ways, the four of us couldn't be any different, and in others we were so alike it was scary. We were all stubborn, ruthless and held grudges. And we all liked it when Kennedy orgasmed.

"You're right," Mannix said softly. "This is bull-shit. We should all be home by now."

I turned my face to look at him. That was the first time I'd ever heard him admit someone else was right. He was in no way admitting he was wrong. He was just agreeing with my assessment of the present situation.

"We'll get there," I told him. "They'll turn up any minute now and we can all get the fuck out of here."

"Yeah." He sagged slightly in the chair, his gaze now on the stained carpet on the floor. "We have to, because I won't lose either of them. I can't."

I turned my face away from his vulnerability. He wouldn't want me to see it. If anyone asked later, I'd swear on anything you put in front of me, that he was stone cold, rock hard the entire time, just like me. Neither of us faltered. Neither of us fell apart.

My eyes once again found the gap in the curtain. I watched the fading daylight. In another hour, it would be dark and we'd have to go in search of food. In the meantime, we waited.

CHAPTER FIVE

KENNEDY

"This is the place." Hunter pulled the car up outside a small block of rundown apartments.

I eyed them doubtfully. I wouldn't put it past the twins to take us somewhere random and leave us here for shits and giggles.

I glanced over at Ice as he nodded.

"This is right." He saw me looking at him and smiled reassuringly.

"Did you think we'd drop you off at the wrong place?" Parker asked. He actually looked offended.

I actually didn't give a shit. "That was exactly what I thought." I undid my seatbelt and opened the door. Thankfully, the door *did* open. For half a second there, I was worried we'd be stuck in here.

Yeah, where these two were concerned, I had

some small trust issues. Not to mention the desire to punch Hunter in the face hadn't diminished much in the drive over. I decided it wasn't worth hurting my hand for, but I wouldn't rule out hurting him at a later date. Or his brother.

"Ouch." Parker looked over the seat at me and pouted, but he didn't look too concerned. If he did, that was too fucking bad. He gave me a long, curious look.

I knew he wanted to insist I tell him what Bell told me. He also knew I wasn't going to tell him jack shit. Even if they hadn't gone along with Lila and handed us over to Bell, I wouldn't have. Honestly, I hadn't even gotten my head around it yet.

I gave Parker a sarcastic smile and stepped out of the car.

Ice climbed out behind me and closed the door. He did that guy thing of tapping the roof of the car to let them know they could drive away, as if the closing of the door wasn't a dead giveaway.

Both twins gave us a cheerful wave before the SUV peeled away from the curb and disappeared into the traffic.

"I'm guessing those two have a short life expectancy," I said dryly.

Ice took my hand and chuckled. "They're useful in their own way. They got us here after all."

"It's also their fault we got caught in the first place," I pointed out. "They didn't have to let Lila boss them around."

He grinned and didn't say anything.

I frowned at him. "Are you suggesting I'm allowed to boss you around?"

He stopped and pressed his lips over mine in a kiss so soft it made my heart flutter. "Any time, Beautiful."

"I'll remember that," I assured him. I briefly wondered if the other two would let me do the same. In the same thought I reminded myself they had to be alive first.

I tipped back my head and looked up at the apartment building. "If they're anywhere, they'll be here?"

"Here or not too far away," he agreed. He didn't say it, but I knew he was thinking the same thing I was. On tender feet, he led me to the elevator and pressed the button for the sixth floor.

The doors slid open to reveal a small, well-used elevator car.

"Imagine how many people have fucked in here." He traced a finger down my cheek as the door closed.

A shiver travelled down my body and to my core.

"I'm guessing a few." My voice sounded choked to my own ears. "Is there a name for that, like the mile high club?"

A frown flitted across his brow. "I have no idea. I'll have to look it up the next time I get my hands on a phone or a computer." He slipped his hand around the back of my head and brought my face to his in a deep, wet kiss. He slipped his other hand up the front of my dress and tugged it down, along with the cup of my bra.

The elevator could stop at another floor at any time, and the door could open, but rather than deterring me, the idea made me more excited.

I reached down to undo his jeans and slid them down just far enough for me to wrap my fingers around his cock.

He grunted and pushed himself into my hands a couple of times.

He pushed up my dress and shoved them and my panties down, before slipping his fingers between my legs and over my pussy. He found my clit and started to work me with quick, deliberate strokes. He had me panting in moments.

"You're so wonderfully wet already." He tugged

my dress up further before he turned me around and bent me over.

He placed his hand between us and guided his cock before slipping it deep into my pussy.

I groaned at a being filled so suddenly and deeply.

"I can't get over how incredible you feel every time," he said breathlessly. He paused for a couple of breaths, then started to pound into me, over and over.

I pressed my palms against the wall to steady myself. The vibrations from the moving elevator passed all the way through my body, adding to the sensations and pushing me closer and closer to the edge.

Light flashed under the doors with each floor we passed.

Second.

I reached down to rub my own sensitive, aching nub. I was so close now.

Third.

Ice thrust harder and harder. "God... Beautiful... Come with me."

Fourth.

I groaned and came hard, clenching his cock and making my fingers damp.

"Holy shit." He stilled and came too, spilling

himself inside me while he grunted and ground himself against me.

Fifth.

He slid out and we hastily fastened our clothes and smoothed them back down into place.

Sixth.

I was straightening my hem when the doors slid open.

"Here we are." He managed to sound like he wasn't panting or out of breath. His cheeks weren't even flushed.

Mine were, I could feel them.

I took a moment to compose myself before I stepped out of the elevator behind him.

We were in another corridor, this one lit by windows which looked like they hadn't been washed in my lifetime.

It was better than total darkness.

I looked at a sign on the wall. "Which number apartment?"

"Nine." He grinned.

I rolled my eyes. "Whose idea was that?"

"Just a lucky coincidence." He shrugged.

I turned to the right and followed the corridor that led to apartment six-nine.

"Who knows about this place?" Just because Bell

let us go didn't mean there wasn't someone waiting to ambush us or fuck knows what else. The fact the evil twins knew made me beyond uneasy.

Ice rubbed the back of his neck. "A handful of us. There are places like this all over the country. Some we know about, many we don't. If we all knew about all of them, they'd be at risk. As for this one, we have to take the chance, or we head home to Dusk Bay." He cocked his head at me questioningly.

I looked from him to the door and back again.

"If anyone is lying in wait for us, they would have seen us arrive," I reasoned.

"If they had cameras in the elevator, they would have seen us come too," he said with a smile.

I made a face at him, then raised my hand to knock on the door.

"Wait, is there a secret knock or something?" For all I knew, I had to knock six times and then nine so they'd know it was us.

"There should be, shouldn't there?" He let his hand drop and slap against his thigh.

"Go ahead and knock." He stepped up next to the door and positioned himself between me and any trouble if trouble opened the door.

I knocked.

We waited.

I knocked again.

The lock clicked and the door opened enough to show it was fastened to the frame with a chain. One that looked more sturdy than the rest of the building.

"Shit."

The door closed and the chain was pulled aside before it opened again. Mannix reached out and grabbed my arm to tug me into the room.

I found myself surrounded by guys and embracing arms. Everyone tried talking at once and you can imagine how well that went.

After a minute or so, Mannix barked, "Everyone, shut the fuck up." He kicked the door shut and waved Ice and me over to the bed.

I sat in the middle. Ice sat on one side, Ares on the other.

Mannix pulled over a chair and flopped down on it. He stared at me and Ice like he couldn't believe we were there in front of him.

Honestly, I felt the same way about him and Ares.

"It's about time you got here," Ares said with a grunt. "Mannix wanted to leave without you. Another hour and we would have left for the airport."

Mannix scowled at him but didn't answer.

Instead he took my hands and asked what happened to us.

In as few words as I could use, I described the room, and the way our plan didn't work the way we hoped.

Ice then did the same.

When he was done, I looked down at the floor. "He let us go because there's something he needs me to do, but I can't tell you until we get back to Dusk Bay. I can only ask you to trust me and hope you don't hate me."

"We could never hate you," Mannix said. "I can insist you tell me and you'll have no choice."

"Don't insist." I looked at him with pleading eyes. This was difficult enough without him going all mafia boss on me. He might say they couldn't hate me, but if they knew what this was about, they might change their minds.

He looked conflicted, but he nodded.

"Fine, but I want to be in on it when you can talk about it." He gave me that look like he expected to be obeyed, no matter what. It was kinda hot, even though he must know it wasn't necessarily that simple.

I quickly realised he did know, he just didn't care. Whatever was going on, he'd be privy to it, or heads would roll. I wondered if anyone ever told him no and got away with it for very long. It was hot, and it was scary.

"I'll make sure you're there," I said finally. "All of you. You deserve to hear it after everything we've been through." I hated to leave them out of the loop, but the loop might wrap around my neck like a noose soon enough.

Mannix's expression softened. "Ares and I didn't go through much compared to you two. That was fucked up and I'll make sure Bell pays for it."

"Can we build a sensory deprivation room?" Ice asked suddenly.

Mannix didn't even hesitate to respond. "Yes. Yes we can. I can think of the perfect first visitor when it's done."

"Me too," I said dryly. "Hunter and Parker Brantley."

"Them too," Ares agreed. "Better make a few of these rooms. We're going to need them."

I couldn't contain a shudder at the idea of going anywhere near another place like that.

Hopefully the guys didn't expect me to check out the handiwork when it was built. I was going to have nightmares about it for a while. I might have to see if I could find a night light in one of the shops in the airport before we flew out. Just a soft one. I didn't think I'd be able to sleep in the dark. Not tonight.

Fuck knows when.

Mannix called for a car to come and pick us up, while Ares dug out some food from the small fridge and made Ice and I sandwiches.

While I ate, I was only too aware of three sets of eyes on me, all wondering what Bell wanted of me.

If they knew, they might cut my throat and leave me here for someone else to find.

CHAPTER SIX

KENNEDY

I'd been confined behind the iron gates of Leo's house before. When they closed behind me this time, there was something eerily final. Like the clang as the two sides met and locked meant I'd never leave.

"You okay?" Ice's hand rested on my thigh. He hadn't left my side since we found the other guys.

Ares and Mannix hadn't gone too far either, but neither had much to say.

Ares, in particular, hadn't said more than a word or two. He kept looking at me with an unreadable expression that could indicate anything from him being happy to see me, to him wishing I was dead.

Our relationship was complicated to say the least.

"Yeah, kind of," I said. As okay as a person could

be when she felt like she was being taken to her execution.

Part of me hoped Leo and Mum were home, so I could get this over with. The rest of me wished they'd gone on an extended vacation around the world so I could put this off indefinitely. A year or two should do it.

"Whatever it is, it's not gonna change how we feel about you," he said softly.

Ares, who sat on the other side of him, looked around him at us both. "Don't count on it. That depends what she has to say or do. If it's nothing too bad, she would have told us by now."

As usual, his accusing words pissed me off.

"That's assuming a lot," I said coolly. "If I could tell you, I would have."

"It's easy to say that when you have no intention of telling us." He smirked.

"You're not going to pressure it out of me." The look I gave him was supposed to be stone cold, but I suspected it came off looking mildly irritated. He knew exactly how to get under my skin. Asshole.

"Enough," Mannix snapped. He looked over the front passenger seat at us and jerked his head towards the driver. The message was clear. Don't argue in front of someone else.

Our business was our business and not for anyone else to overhear.

Ares slumped back in his seat and crossed his arms, but he gave me a last look like this conversation wasn't over.

I sighed. As far as I was concerned, it was more than over. Until we got back into the house.

"Whatever it is, we'll deal with it," Ice whispered. "Like we deal with everything else."

"By killing people?" I was only half joking.

"If we have to," he said. "Whatever it takes, we've got you. Right, Ares?" He turned his face and gave the other guy a look.

"If you say so," Ares grunted.

The driver pulled the car into the garage. The door rolled shut behind us.

The clang of metal hitting concrete was louder and more final than the gates.

A layer of sweat on my palms, I pushed open the car door and got out.

Ice scrambled after me. Mannix stepped out of the front passenger seat and put a possessive hand on my lower back. With Ares trailing behind, they led me inside.

"There you are!" Mum's voice bordered on shrill

the moment we stepped into the enormous kitchen. "I was starting to worry."

The next thing I knew, she had her arms around me, hugging me and kissing my cheek.

"I'm fine," I protested. I hugged her back for a minute before untangling myself from her. "Is Leo here?"

She leaned back, her brow creased. "Yes, he's in his office. Why? Do you need to—"

"I'll get him," Mannix said. He looked at me like he'd prefer not to let me out of his sight, but trotted off, his back stiff.

Mum led me over to the couch and sat me down. "What is this about? Are you sure you're all right?"

Before I could answer, Ice said, "I'll make some coffee."

"Good idea." I could use a cup or two. Didn't prisoners on death row get a last request? This was mine.

Wait, should I have asked for a bottle of vodka instead? Oh well, it was too late for that.

I caught Ares's eye as the blond god leaned against the wall, arms crossed, one foot pressed against the wall behind him. He wore the same expression he had since we were at the apartment. Guarded, watching. He reminded me of a lion biding his time while he waited for an opportunity to leap on his prey. Or a hunter who set a trap and sat back until it was set off.

And me, I felt like a little mouse who was too enticed by the cheese. Any moment now, the trap would snap and I'd be caught in that snare forever. Unable to run or fight or flee.

His eyes lingered on me, but he looked away at the sound of approaching footsteps.

I followed the sound as Leo and Mannix stepped into the room.

Judging by the look on Leo's face, Mannix had filled him in briefly. He clearly still had questions and was expecting answers. Did they realise how alike they were? Neither of them were good at taking no for an answer. Come to think of it, none of us were.

Leo got straight to the point.

"I hear things didn't go to plan."

Ares snorted.

"Things went sideways," Mannix said. "But we got in and out alive."

"Thank goodness you did," Mum said. She put an arm around my shoulders and squeezed.

Leo looked less impressed. He would have preferred if we'd succeeded.

Me too.

I half-listened as Mannix filled him in, going into detail every step of the way. More detail than I would have thought to give. Honestly, more detail than I'd noticed. From the exact time we stepped foot in Bell's mansion, to how long it took us to get to his office.

Mannix described the layout of the office, down to the clock on the wall. He didn't mention fucking me on the desk, but he left out nothing else. Either he had a photographic memory or he paid more attention than I did.

Leo listened carefully, asking questions here and there, but mostly absorbing what his son said, taking mental notes. Probably planning something else against Bell based on what we found there. That was inevitable.

Mannix finished with him and Ares getting separated from me and Ice.

Ice took over from there, describing how we met up with the twins and then Lila Bell. How she'd assumed Hunter and Parker apprehended us for her and, at gunpoint, took us back to her father.

Leo looked furious. If the Brantley twins were in front of him, he'd probably bang their heads together until they were a bloodied mess.

I'd be inclined to help him.

My coffee was almost cold before I remembered it was in my hand. I drank it anyway. Why waste perfectly good coffee?

Ice mentioned himself being chained to the ceiling for a while, but made it sound like it was nothing too terrible. Apart from being bored, the experience didn't seem to have had a lasting impact.

I wished I was half as tough as he was. Or half as crazy. Whatever it was he had going on, I wanted some of it. Especially right now.

My heart galloped in my chest like it was trying to escape the rest of me.

Get out while you can. I was surprised no one could hear it. It pounded so hard it hurt.

All eyes turned to me while I described the basement room. The one good thing about it was that there wasn't much to describe. Metal door, stone walls, darkness, soundproof.

I was done in a sentence or two.

That was the easy part behind me though.

I told them about Chloe opening the door and letting me out. I told them she seemed a lot more sympathetic than Lila had. 'Seemed,' being the key word here.

No one in the room seemed inclined to cut her

any slack. After all, she was a Bell. That made her just as suspect as Lila.

I considered pointing out that they supported Reuben and Caleb Brantley, in spite of Hunter and Parker being a pair of pricks. Since that wouldn't go down as well, I decided not to bother.

I described the steps up to the main house, trying to be as detailed as Mannix, but they were steps. Tread, riser, tread, riser. Concrete. A crack here or there. There wasn't much to tell.

I closed my eyes and thought back before describing the walk from the basement steps to Bell's office.

"There were more guards around than there were when we went in," I said slowly.

Ice grinned. "We must have given them a scare."

"We rarely send anyone directly into places like that," Leo said. "They don't usually end well." His eyebrows dropped. He seemed to be thinking of something in particular. This was far from his first rodeo. How many people had he sent to their death?

If I had to guess, I'd say a non-zero number. Maybe so many another four wouldn't have mattered, even if one was his son.

Mannix gave him a dark look.

Leo hadn't hesitated to send his younger son straight into the lion's den.

Although, Mannix insisted on going. He knew the risks when he led us in there. He calculated those versus the reward and decided it was worth it.

We all had. We knew there was a chance we wouldn't walk out of there. Maybe it was rash, but we all went in with our eyes open. If we had it to do over again, would we?

Probably, but next time we'd succeed.

"Luckily, this did end well," Mum said. "I don't know what I'd do if anything bad happened to my baby girl." She then proceeded to give every guy in the room look like it was one hundred percent their fault I was in danger at all.

I pressed my mouth into a line. I was as much to blame as they were, but she had to wear some of it herself. She dragged me into this life to begin with.

"We wouldn't have let anything happen to Kennedy," Mannix growled.

I looked down at the floor.

"Definitely not," Ice agreed.

"Cut to the chase," Ares snapped.

All eyes turned to him, including mine.

"Kennedy has something to say." He nodded to me. "Spit it the fuck out."

Now everyone was looking at me instead.

Ugh.

"What is it?" Mum asked. Her brow was creased with maternal worry.

She cared, I knew she did, but part of me was so angry with her I wanted to hurl the last couple of mouthfuls of my coffee in her face.

"Samuel Bell let me go," I said just loud enough for everyone in the room to hear. "He let Ice and I go because he wanted me to give you a message."

I looked directly at my mother.

She looked confused, then her face paled. "You don't have to—"

"Yes, I do." I exhaled out my nose and looked around at everyone. These were the last moments these words went unsaid, and I wanted to make them last. Once they were gone, they were gone forever.

"Samuel Bell said he knows he's my father."

CHAPTER SEVEN

KENNEDY

The silence was like a void after a thunder crack.

My mother sat stunned. Her face was white with a little green.

The only sound in the room was the tick of the clock on the wall. It counted down the seconds. A minute. Two minutes.

Finally the silence was broken by Ares's low exclamation.

"What the fuck?"

I looked over at him, expecting to see hatred in his eyes. I saw surprise. No doubt when it sank in...

Leo sounded dazed. "Helen?"

Trembling, she turned to him.

"It was... It was..." she stammered.

He seemed to rally, pulling himself together in the face of my words.

"It was what?" he said carefully.

"It was a long time ago." Her eyes were wide. She was scrambling for the words and maybe something to cling onto.

"Did he rape you?" Leo's question was direct, his face tinged with pink. He obviously hadn't decided how to respond. Her answer would guide him.

"No," she said quickly. Then more softly and slowly, "No. It was at Brutham. We had a...connection."

Ares snorted. "Obviously."

She ignored him.

"I think we both knew it couldn't go anywhere but we gave in to temptation. Then we both graduated and went our separate ways. A couple of months later, I realised I was pregnant. I never told him. I put him out of my mind and moved on."

"So it's true?" I whispered. Until then, I wasn't sure. In the back of my mind, I expected her to deny it. To laugh at the absurdity of the suggestion. To tell me it was just a mindfuck from Bell. The truth knocked the breath out of my lungs for a while.

Somehow, I managed to put together coherent thoughts and words. And an accusing tone to match.

"You told me my father left because he wanted to be with someone else." All my life I thought maybe I did something wrong. Something so horrible it made him leave. I'd wondered if there was something I could have said or done that might have made him stay. Maybe if I was better behaved. Cried less. *Something*.

Now I knew why I didn't remember him. Before yesterday, we'd never met.

Mum sighed. "It was complicated. Then, when I started to work for the Brantleys, it became more complicated. It was better if no one knew. I didn't mean to deceive anyone. I thought it was for the best."

"But he knew," Leo said coldly. "He did the maths and he knew. You were never married?"

"Not to him, no," Mum said quickly. "Even if I told him..." She shook her head. "His family had plans for him. He was always going to marry Penelope. Chloe and Lila's mother."

"Would you have married him if you could?" I asked. How different would my life be if she had? Would I be a coldhearted minion like his daughter Lila? My *sister* Lila.

I hadn't let myself think about that yet. I had two younger sisters. One happy to lock me up, the other happy to let me out. Or at least, happy to follow orders.

Figured my family would be as dysfunctional as fuck.

"I don't know," Mum admitted. "It doesn't matter now; that's the past. It's done."

"It matters because if you were married when Kennedy was born, she would have been the legitimate heir to the Bell family and everything that goes with that," Leo said.

His eyes settled on me.

I knew what he was getting at. If that happened, we'd be mortal enemies. In theory.

"Including two ambitious younger sisters who are prepared to tear each other apart to be heads of the family, much less you," Mannix said.

If I thought Ares was unreadable, he was nothing to Mannix's expression right now. I had literally no idea what was going through his head.

It was absolutely terrifying.

"I, for one, don't care," Ice said lightly, sweetly. He came to sit down on the other side of me and put his arm over my shoulders.

"Firstly, Kennedy is still Kennedy, regardless of who her sperm donor was. Secondly, if she wants to start going by Knight-Bell, I'm all for it. It sounds badass. Like, don't ask for whom the night bell tolls, for it tolls for thee." He grinned.

I shook my head at him.

"I think my life expectancy might be reduced somewhat if I go by Bell."

If the expression on Leo's face was any indication, the jury was still out on my life expectancy as it was. If he wasn't impressed by Chloe being nice to me, then he'd be unmoved by our existing relationship being a more or less positive one.

My relationships with the guys in particular. Leo could just as easily withdraw his blessing.

"I don't care either," Mannix declared finally. "Kennedy is ours regardless of who her father might be." He shot Mum a look, clearly laying every drop of blame firmly in her lap.

"Bell has no claim on her, especially if he knew she existed all this time and didn't bother to say so. That includes his spawn. If they think otherwise, they'll have to go through us."

Ice jerked his thumb towards Mannix. "What he said."

Ares grunted something that might have been an agreement.

I managed a faint smile for all of them, but my eyes still found Leo's. At the end of the day, if he

would have come out sooner or later. That fact simplified nothing, did nothing to make me feel better about everything. What other truth bombs would land before this was done?

"Not a *loving* father, no," Leo agreed. "I wouldn't put anything past Samuel Bell. His daughters knew exactly where to find that room, didn't they?"

My lips dropped apart and I nodded.

Fuck, what kind of monster was he? Torturing a stranger, especially someone who did wrong by you, was one thing. Locking your own child in a place like that—that was horrible.

"The father of the year award *doesn't* go to Samuel Bell," Ice said.

"No, it doesn't," Mannix agreed. He looked at Leo, clearly wondering if he'd qualify. Leo's response to me would be the answer to that.

Leo all but ignored him. "Bell also sent that man after you."

I stared. "Frank Nixon. He wanted to strike out at you."

"Or me," Mum said softly. "It might have been retribution for not telling him about Kennedy."

"It was Bell being an asshole," Mannix said. "He doesn't need a reason. He could come after any one of us, or all of us, because he feels like it. One day it might be about retribution, the next day it might be because he ran out of toilet paper."

"That would be a bummer," Ice said, his expression deadpan.

Ares snorted again. That seemed to be the only method of communication he was capable of right now.

That was relatable. I was having a hard time putting words or thoughts together too.

"What...happens now?" I asked tentatively.

"Nothing happens now," Mannix said without hesitation. "You go on being you. Nothing has to change."

As if he hadn't spoken, Leo said, "Did Bell give you any indication if his daughters knew?"

I frowned and went over everything he said, and everything they said, in my mind.

"He didn't," I said eventually, "but that doesn't necessarily mean they don't. Either Lila knew or she hated me on sight. Either Chloe knew or she felt sorry for me. They didn't give away much. Certainly no more than that."

I pinched the bridge of my nose. "If I had to guess, I'd say they don't know. I'm not basing that on anything in particular though, they just didn't seem very...sisterly."

"I'd operate under the assumption that if they didn't know before, he's told them," Leo said. "And even though you're not the legitimate heir, they may not see it that way."

I pinched a little harder. "Wonderful, I made enemies just by existing."

"Welcome to my world," Mannix said dryly. "All the more reason we're going to stick together. Right, Dad?"

Leo regarded his son for approximately an hour or two.

Okay, it wasn't more than a couple of minutes. He had a way of keeping people on the edge until he was good and ready to pull them in or push them off.

"Kennedy is still my stepdaughter, and I'll do everything in my power to keep her safe as the rest of us. However—" he raised an eyebrow at me, "—if I see any indication that you're working against us, I won't hesitate."

He didn't need to elaborate, we knew what he meant. He'd kill me and not blink. Not regret it.

"I have no intention of working against any of you," I assured him. "All I want right now is to finish my degree, run my gym and eventually my own cyber security business."

"I strongly advise keeping your head down for a

while," Leo said. "This may blow over and it may not. You might have to get used to being inside the fence for quite some time. And if you go outside, you're not going alone."

"No, she's not," Mannix agreed. "Kennedy will have someone with her at all times."

I sighed. "Please tell me you'll let me go to the toilet alone."

"At all times," he repeated. "From now on, there's only four people I trust. That doesn't include any of the staff." He didn't add that my mother wasn't included, that was obvious.

She kept something important from us all this time, that made her suspicious at best.

I wasn't sure I could trust her anymore. If she lied about my father, what else did she lie about? If it wasn't for the obvious resemblance and the red hair, I'd wonder if she was actually my mother.

"I really think you should consider calling yourself Kennedy Knight-Bell," Ice said.

Obviously he wanted to break up a tense moment. It worked to some extent. I managed half a chuckle and the mood lightened slightly.

I swatted him on the arm. "Not a chance." If my younger sisters didn't know about me before, they would if I went around calling myself that. It occurred to me that if somehow Lila married one of the Brantley twins, I'd be related to those assholes too.

Ugh, this kept getting better.

Of course, I'd also be related to Zeke Brantley, but at this point I didn't think that would be worth it. I'd need front row tickets to Wolf Venom concerts for life, even to make it slightly better. Not to mention a lifetime of backstage passes and tour merch.

"If it's okay, I'd like a long soak in the bath, and then some sleep." I tried to stifle a yawn but failed. The last couple of days were exhausting and I was over them.

"Of course," Mum said. "You must be tired after everything you've been through and done. We're so impressed with you."

I could only manage a watery smile for her. At some point I'd forgive her, but not right now. Right now, I had a bunch of stuff to figure out and come to terms with.

"Kennedy." It was the first word Ares said since we were in the car. "I want to talk."

He'd given me no indication of his thoughts on my paternity. I had a feeling I was about to get every detail and I may not want to hear what he had to say.

CHAPTER EIGHT

ARES

I ignored the looks from everyone else and took her up to my room.

I grabbed her arm in a grip that was intended to be bruising, and pushed her inside before I locked the door behind us.

I shoved her over to my bed and down on her ass before I stepped away. I paced a few steps, then turned around to face her.

She looked at me with a combination of fear and defiance. Mostly defiance. Good, that was exactly what I wanted from her. She was no damsel in distress. I wanted her to stand up to me, but I also needed her to know exactly how I was feeling.

"Ares—"

"Shut up," I snapped. I curled my hands into fists.

"This is fucked up. Everything about this is fucked up." I slammed a fist against my thigh. Revelled in the shooting pain. It wasn't enough.

"You think I don't—" she started again.

"I said shut up," I growled. "Shut up and listen."

She glared at me, but sat back and rested her hands in her lap.

I exhaled and closed my eyes for a moment. "I grew up with *nothing*. We were lucky to get more than a meal a day. Everything was secondhand at best. I went to school in a uniform that should have been thrown out years ago. Too big, too small, whatever. Nothing ever fit right. Every item of clothing I got had some other kid's name on the label. If I was lucky, I'd find a jumper in the lost and found. If I wasn't lucky, I was cold."

I opened my eyes but didn't look at her. The last thing I wanted to see on her face was pity. It was a shitty past but that was what it was, the past. As far as I was concerned, I'd say this, then never talk about it again.

"Then I met Mannix and Ice. He went by Isaac then, until one of our teachers kept pronouncing it Ice-aac, instead of Ize-aac. We started calling him that too. At some point, it changed to Ice."

I closed my eyes and shook my head at the

memory. Life seemed a lot simpler back then. Even when my family had nothing.

I looked at her now to see a faint smile on her lips. Fuck, she was gorgeous. The red hair and freckles really did it for me.

"The three of us were inseparable from the moment we met," I said. "I don't remember when, but at some point I became aware of what Mannix's family was all about. That included money and power. Two things my family had none of. Two things I wanted desperately. And all I had to do to get it was hate the Bell family."

I glanced down at the floor. The carpet was clean. So clean. Anywhere I lived as a kid, it was always covered in stains. Fuck only knew what from, but there were plenty of them. Never here though. If anything was dropped on the carpet, it was cleaned. If it didn't come out, Leo would probably have it ripped out and replaced. Fucking rich people.

"If I tried to think back to a time when I didn't hate Samuel Bell and his family, his whole organisation, I wouldn't find one. It's deeply ingrained. It's part of who I am."

I looked back up at her. Her expression was wary now.

Yeah, I'd be wary of me too.

"And here you fucking are." I waved a fisted hand in her direction. "You're one of them. Samuel Bell's fucking daughter. His blood runs in your veins, and I fucking hate it. I *hate* it."

I stalked over to her, shoved her onto her back and straddled her thighs.

"No part of you should be his," I growled. "Every part of you is *mine*." I wanted to tear her apart, pull out any bit of her that was from him and put her back together again. Cleansed of any traces of taint.

I wrapped my fingers around her throat and squeezed. "Every part."

The defiance hadn't left her eyes. It made my cock rock hard. She tilted her chin back and met my gaze, unwavering.

That made me angrier than ever.

I grabbed the front of her shirt and ripped it apart, the two pieces falling away from her body. I tossed them aside and tugged the straps of her bra off her shoulders. I pulled it until it was down around her waist, exposing her beautiful, milky breasts.

With no mercy whatsoever, I drew one of her nipples between my teeth and bit hard enough to make her cry out. The sound was like music. Better than music. It was desperate, erotic sin.

I bit the other one even harder, then bit all

around her breasts. Not enough to draw blood, but enough to leave bruises and marks. My marks, to show everyone she was mine.

I climbed off her, sat beside her while I undid her shorts and yanked them down her legs. She wore little black lace panties that made the most satisfying sound when I ripped them off her body. I tossed them over my shoulder, then slammed her onto her stomach to unhook her bra.

I grabbed her wrists and all but dragged her up my bed, where I kept straps attached to the headboard. I looked her in the eyes as I bound first one wrist, then the other. Nice and tight.

I leaned in to whisper in her ear. "The safe word is koala." I was full of fury, but not blinded enough to be unaware that she may need to put limits to what I was about to do. I was an asshole, not an abuser.

She nodded but didn't make a sound.

I reached into a drawer and pulled out a paddle. Not the gentle, padded kind with velvet or whatever shit people used. The panel itself was hard leather, the handle smooth, well worn wood.

Channelling every drop of hatred for the blood that violated her veins, I brought the paddle hard down on her ass.

She cried out in pain and surprise, but didn't say a word. Didn't ask me to stop.

I waited a moment, watching as her cheek turned a beautiful shade of red.

I smiled to myself. She was a work of art. A beautiful sculpture under my hands. Mine to shape and shade however I wanted.

I wanted, needed more.

I brought the paddle down again and again on her tender flesh. Her ass turned redder and redder. Every ounce of fury went into every spank, as though I could beat the Bell out of her.

Over and over until I lost count. My breath came out in pants. My cock was so hard I thought it might burst.

Finally, when I was almost out of steam, she patted the mattress beside her and in a muffled voice, said, "Koala."

I immediately threw the paddle onto the floor and rolled her over onto her back. Tears poured down her cheeks, but she hadn't lost even a drop of defiance.

I wiped the tears off her chin with my thumb and asked, "Who do you belong to?"

"Mannix, and Ice, and you," she said softly.

"Hell yeah you do." I pressed a hand down

between her thighs and over her drenched pussy. "You're so wet. You liked getting spanked, didn't you?"

"Yeah, I did." She cleared her throat. Composed herself and lifted her chin. "But now I want you to fuck me."

She gave me a challenging look, reminding me of our conversation a few weeks ago. The one where she pointed out that I said *when* I fuck her, not *if*. I'd also told her I'd give her pain. I'd done that.

I thought about taunting her. leaving without fucking her, just so she couldn't be right. But my cock was so hard, I was surprised it hadn't broken my zipper to escape.

"You do, huh?" I wasn't going to torture myself, but wasn't going to make it that easy for her either. "What does a good girl say when she wants to be fucked?"

"Shut the fuck up and give me that dick like a good boy?" she teased.

I snorted a laugh, but pulled off my jeans and boxers and straddled her again.

"If you think I'm a good boy, you don't know me well enough." I gripped the hem of my T-shirt with one hand and pulled it off my head. "Because I'm very, very bad."

I pried apart her knees with my thighs, smiling at her wince of pain. She was going to feel that spanking for days. Now I was going to fuck her hard enough for her to feel me inside her for even longer.

Her arms still restrained above her head, she had no choice but to lie there while I positioned my cock and slipped my tip inside her body. Then a little more.

"Fucking hell," I murmured. I was bigger than the other guys and she was nice and tight. I stopped halfway in to let her get used to me. Her muscles squeezed me like a clamp. A hot, wet clamp.

She moaned, her eyes wide. "You're so big. Holy..."

"You can take me." Whether she liked it or not.

I pushed myself in further. Her muscles resisted, but I kept pressing and pressing until I was all the way inside her gorgeous body.

"There we go, good girl. You were made for my cock."

She seemed to be beyond words and right now. So was I.

I rested inside her for a minute or so, then started to thrust. Slowly at first, then increasing in speed until I was pounding in as hard as I could.

I reached in under her knees and lifted her legs

over my shoulders so I could slam in deeper. With every stroke, my tip hit her inner wall.

"Oh my..." Her upper body twisted and writhed against the restraints. Her nipples looked as hard as my cock. Her breathing was ragged. She was close to coming.

I managed to muster the words to say, "Tell me what you want."

She moaned. "I want to come. I need to."

"Is that all you want?" I slowed my thrusts to even, deliberate strokes.

"I want you to come too," she said, her face screwed up in concentration. "I want you to come inside me."

"What else?" I pressed.

She panted. "I want you to fill me with your cum. Please..."

"Come for me," I told her. "I want your pussy to come around my cock. And then I'll fill you up, so full you'll overflow."

Her back arched and she screamed as she came hard, her beautiful muscles contracting around my erection, stealing the last of my self control and making me come just as hard. My stomach tensed, then my balls, before I exploded inside her. Filling her as I promised I would.

She milked me for every drop. By the time I sagged across her, I was dry on the inside, but coated with sweat on the outside.

It took me a couple of minutes to catch my breath. Gently, I lowered her legs back down to the mattress and untied her hands. I put my arms around her and drew her to me, my body slick against hers.

"You're mine," I whispered. "No one is going to take you away from me. You belong to me. I love you."

Her body stiffened and for a moment I thought she'd laugh, or say something sarcastic. Finally, mercifully, she relaxed.

"I love you too. Even though you're literally a pain in my ass."

I chuckled against her hair. "You enjoyed every minute of it."

She exhaled at the same time as she spoke. "Yeah, I did. Let's do it again once my skin has healed."

I had every intention of doing just that, but she'd need a while to recover from my anger. Anger which was dissipated now, thanks to her. I couldn't remember a time in my life when I felt as peaceful as I did right now. I could have lain here forever with her in my arms. But then, what kind of boyfriend would I be?

"I'll draw you a bath and pick you out some bath bombs." I couldn't spank her and not take care of her afterward. After all, it would help her to heal more quickly so we could do it again.

No way it had anything to do with me being nice. Not for a second.

CHAPTER NINE

KENNEDY

I winced as I slipped onto a stool.

Should I be horrified Ares took his anger out on me? Maybe, but I'd found his fury arousing. It was another piece of the puzzle that continued to prove I wasn't as normal as I thought I was.

Or maybe this was normal and people didn't talk about it.

Whatever, this was *my* normal.

Think whatever you like, I was grateful to Ares. In some way, I felt I'd violated this place by being here, given who my father was. Ares gave me my punishment. Now I was cleansed. The self-loathing that tried to creep up on me, was gone.

Replaced with pain every time I sat down.

I wouldn't be forgetting last night anytime soon.

My mother walked into the kitchen in time to see the expression on my face.

"Are you all right, sweetheart?" she asked.

She was my mother, of course she was concerned about me.

Today, that concern irritated me.

I picked up my spoon and dug it into my rice bubbles with a vengeance.

"I'm fine," I said coolly.

She sighed and placed her hands palms down in front of me. "You have every right to be confused about everything."

I swear I tried to keep my eyes from rolling, but they acted without my consent.

"I'm not confused, Mum. All my life you lied to me about who my father was. You kept on lying when you brought me here, right to his enemy. Right to where I could get stalked and attacked. And because that wasn't enough, you let me go there, knowing my own father might kill me."

Yeah, I wasn't confused, I was pissed the fuck off.

"I don't think of him that way," she argued. Like somehow that would make everything better.

"Neither does he, apparently." I left my spoon in

my cereal and leaned my elbows on the bench. "He didn't exactly welcome me with open arms and fatherly love."

"He didn't kill you," she pointed out. "He would have if he hadn't known who you were."

"Is that supposed to make me feel better? Daddy's way of showing me love is not killing me? That's at least a thousand kinds of fucked up."

"Watch your language," she snapped. "You have to appreciate the position I was in."

As far as I was concerned, I didn't have to appreciate anything, but I pressed my lips together and listened to what she had to say.

"I was barely older than you and pregnant by a guy I could never be with. I cared about him, even though I knew what he was like. Sam was very much like your three boys are right now. Arrogant, possessive, controlling. Why do you think I warned you about them?"

Without waiting for a response she continued, "I don't want you to end up in the same position I did. Pregnant and alone. If you think for a second those boys will stick around if you—"

I couldn't hear any more without interrupting. "First of all, I'm not going to get pregnant. Secondly, none of them would abandon me if I did. Just because things didn't work out for you doesn't mean they won't work out for me." It didn't mean they would either, but the guys would never turn their backs on their child. Their pride wouldn't let them, even if their possessive natures would.

She looked at me like she thought I was a naïve child.

She sighed. "I don't want to argue with you, Kennedy. I made a mistake and I've done everything in my power to make up for it."

She scratched her perfectly shaped eyebrow. "I figured sooner or later he'd realise there was a chance you were his. I thought once he knew that, he'd take you away from me. So I got in as deep as I could with the people who wouldn't let that happen. In the process, I fell in love with Leo. I knew if you were here, with us, you'd be safe from him. I didn't count on all the other things that happened, and for that I'm sorry, but when you're a parent, all you can do is your best and hope you don't mess it up."

"So I was a mistake?" I asked softly. Of all the things she said, that was one thing my brain decided to fixate on.

Her mouth moved as she scrambled to find the right answer to make me feel better.

"Getting pregnant was a mistake, but having you was the best thing I ever did. Keeping you away from Samuel Bell was the second best thing."

"Did you ever think that if you told him, he'd want to be with you?" Surely that crossed her mind?

She lowered her elbow to the bench and rested her head on her hand. "I thought about it, of course I did, but I knew it wasn't possible. And, to be honest, I wasn't sure it was what I wanted. Like I said, he was ruthless and driven. We never would have lasted and he wouldn't let me leave with you. You were more important to me than any man. Than any other relationship I've ever had."

I couldn't resist asking the question. "Would you leave Leo if I needed you to?"

She didn't meet my eyes.

"I didn't think so." I picked up my spoon again. "I'll do my best not to put you in that position. I'm angry with you, but I know you two love each other and I support you, no matter what."

Unless Leo wanted me dead, in which case I withdrew any and all support, past, present and future.

"Is this where you ask me to support your choice, no matter what?" She straightened up and looked at me through knitted brows.

"I don't need your approval, but if you want to give it, then yeah." I shrugged one shoulder. "I'll take it."

"Why does it hurt you to sit?" she asked.

"You don't want to know," I shot back immediately. "But I can assure you everything was fully consensual."

She grimaced. "It better be, because no one does pissed off like a mother whose baby was hurt."

I resisted making a snide comment about her hurting me. At the end of the day, I got where she was coming from. If I'd had a fling with someone like Hunter or Parker Brantley, for example, and fell pregnant, I'd run and hide too. Not that I would sleep with either of them. Ewww.

Watching Bell get more and more powerful, and knowing there was even a slight possibility he'd take her child away, must have been terrifying.

No, it wasn't that surprising she accepted the safe harbour the Brantley family offered.

When I thought about it, it all made a whole bunch of sense. I just wished I knew sooner.

Or did I?

Would I have gone to Sydney knowing he was my father? Would I have snuck around his house, trying to stay away from him and his other daughters?

No, I would have tried to sneak a peek at at least one of them, to satisfy my curiosity about my roots. And, when Lila caught us, I might have blurted out the truth to try to save myself. I doubted she would have welcomed me with open arms. A bullet in the head seemed more likely.

The reality was, if everyone knew, I wouldn't have stepped foot in this house in the first place. I never would have met the guys. I never would have gone to Bell's. I would have stayed at uni and kept an eye out over my shoulder, in case he or one of the Brantley clan came after me. I would have spent the rest of my life making sure I never had my back to an open door, always nervous walking past a window.

Now everyone knew, but I had people around who wanted to keep me safe.

"I'm sorry you had to find out the way you did," she said, breaking through my thoughts. "If I suspected for a minute what would happen, I would have... I dunno. Stopped you from going? Told you myself? *Something*."

I swallowed a mouthful of rice bubbles. "It is what it is. There's no point beating yourself up about it."

"That's what I have you for," she said jokingly.

As if to prove her point, I poked her in the arm with the handle of my spoon.

"Ouch." She laughed and rubbed her arm.

"Something's been bothering me," I said slowly. "You said he wouldn't have let you leave with me."

"He was always very possessive of his possessions." She wrinkled her nose.

"He was quick enough to let me leave yesterday." I lightly tapped the back of the spoon against the rim of the bowl. "He didn't seem interested in a long, drawn out family reunion or anything like that."

Mum frowned.

"In fact, he seemed more interested in me delivering my message to you." I watched carefully as her frown deepened. "Maybe you don't know him as well as you thought you did. Or as well as you did back then." People change, and twenty-something years was a long time.

She shook her head. "No, it means something. He never does anything without some kind of intent. He let you come back here, knowing he could change that anytime he wants to."

Her expression made my blood run cold. It went colder still when her words sank in.

"You think he might come after me and try to... what? Bring me back into the fold?"

She shook her head. "I honestly have no idea what he might intend. From what I've seen over the years, he's unpredictable at best. Determined and as ruthless and arrogant as ever, at worst."

"And you question my taste in men," I muttered. She could be talking about any of the guys. In them, it was hot. In someone like Samuel Bell, it was terrifying.

She laughed humourlessly. "Being young and silly makes you do young, silly things. You may look back one day and wonder what you ever saw in those boys."

"Not a chance," I said. I wasn't letting them go. They weren't going to let me go. We were in this together, no matter what.

One side of her mouth drew back. "You say that now—"

I cut her off. "I say that now and forever. I know you're not their biggest fan, but when you get to know them you'll realise how amazing they are." I hoped she had no intention of asking me to choose between them and her, because she may not win.

"I hope you're right," she said warily. "In the meantime, be careful and keep your eyes out for anything or anyone out of place. It may be that he's mellowed in his older age, or that he's put his other daughters first, but I wouldn't put anything past him. He has a long memory and holds a grudge."

Well, wasn't that fucking great?

"I should finish eating, I need to get to work." Assuming no one blew the place up in my absence.

CHAPTER TEN

KENNEDY

Nothing in Dusk Bay looked out of place. As far as I could tell, nothing was blown up, nothing imploded. None of the buildings disappeared into a random sinkhole.

None of that helped put a dent in my unease. On the contrary, it grew the closer we got to the gym.

I was ready to put it down to a healthy dose of paranoia, until I looked over at Mannix.

He watched out the window with narrowed eyes, taking in everything, his lips pressed tight together. A day or two of stubble made him look older, sexier. An air of barely contained violence hung over him.

He was the alpha male, the apex predator ready to hunt, ready to kill. His prey— anyone who got in his way.

In his present mood, even I would step aside. He wouldn't hurt me, not deliberately, but he was dangerous, and anyone who forgot that, even for a moment, was a dumbass.

Or a corpse.

"What is it?" I asked softly.

He responded with a shake of his head so slight I would have missed it if I wasn't watching.

"I don't know. Something. Don't let your guard down. The minute we do, we're fucked." His fingers closed over the gun he kept at his hip, hidden by his shirt.

"I wasn't planning to. When do I get one of those?"

"You don't," he replied. "Having a gun makes you a target."

"What does having one make you?" I asked. Hadn't I already proved I was no shrinking violet? In spite of what Mum said about Bell potentially coming after me, I was determined to stand up for myself.

Naturally, the guys had other ideas, so here I was in the back of the SUV, being driven to work in the company of all three of them. None of them seemed inclined to let me out of their sight.

This couldn't be their lives until the end of time,

could it? Guarding me twenty-four hours a day, seven days a week. I didn't mind the company, but they had their own lives to live. Sooner or later, they'd start to resent me. That would end us faster than anything Bell might do.

"It makes me someone who knows how to use one," Mannix said. "And when. Don't worry about it, we've got you."

That sounded very much like, 'Don't worry your pretty little head about it, us menfolk will take on all the bears while you traipse around the kitchen, barefoot and pregnant.'

I bristled.

"Maybe I want to have me too," I snapped. "Maybe I want to be able to protect you guys if I need to."

He gave me a look that said both, 'don't argue with me,' and that he was sceptical about being protected by a woman. Or by me, anyway.

"I think Kennedy is right," Ice said. "She did well with a gun in Sydney. I don't see any reason she shouldn't have one now. Although, it might be dangerous to do gymnastics when you're packing. You might do a backsault and shoot yourself in the foot."

"Lucky I'm not stupid enough to do something

like that," I said dryly. What was it with the guys today? Were they being particularly sexist, or was I touchier than usual?

Possibly both. After what we went through, it made sense we were on edge, but I didn't like us taking it out on each other.

"Are you sure about that?" Ares asked. He looked around from the front passenger seat and smirked.

I flipped him off.

Even after saying, 'I love you,' to each other, he was still the same old Ares. Sarcastic, smug asshole. Exactly the way I liked him. I would have hated it if he changed or walked on eggshells around me. It seemed we were destined to be affectionately antago-nistic towards each other. I was here for it.

"I wouldn't do anything that stupid," I said. "I'll leave doing dumb shit to you."

He narrowed his eyes at me. "Bitch."

I smiled. "Asshole."

"Red Riding Pussy." His eyes shone.

"Banana Head." If he was going to insult my hair colour, I'd insult his.

Ice laughed. "Banana Head. That's hilarious."

"Fuck off," Ares told him. "Bun Head."

Ice snorted, clearly not offended in the slightest. "I've been called worse than that."

"Is that a challenge?" Mannix asked.

"That depends, do you dare to accept it?" Ice asked. He glanced at Mannix in the rearview mirror.

"I dare," Mannix agreed. "But let me get back to you on that. We're almost at the gym. More focusing, less thinking up creative nicknames and insults. For the record, I think Banana Head is perfect." A smile tugged at the corners of his mouth but didn't quite come to fruition.

"You can fuck off too," Ares said, but he turned his attention back outside the SUV.

I met Mannix's gaze and grinned. Yes, it was dangerous to get distracted, but for a minute or two it was nice to forget about everything but insulting Ares. After all, the more I insulted him, the better the punishment he gave me for it. The thought made my pussy throb. Fortunately my t-shirt covered the bruises all over my breasts from his teeth. It would take time before those faded away.

In the meantime, I wore them like badges of honour.

Ice pulled the car up in front of the gym and put it in park.

Like everywhere else, nothing looked out of place, but the feeling of unease increased.

There was definitely something very fucking wrong here.

I stepped out of the car. The hair on my arms stood on end as though they too were at high alert.

The guys hurried to surround me.

I wanted to tell them to disperse and behave like normal human beings, but given the way my senses tingled, I might be better off with them around me. All three had their hands near their guns.

I pulled out the key and unlocked the door to the gym.

Pushed it open.

I saw him immediately.

"Fucking hell."

Charlie stood at an awkward angle, leaning heavily to the right. Around his neck, the silk which hung from the ceiling was wrapped tight. His eyes were open, staring at nothing. His hands were by his sides, as though someone held him down, or he hadn't tried to fight back.

He was definitely dead. For a while, by the look of him.

I put a hand over my mouth. "How long—" I looked over at Ice. If anyone was able to tell how long Charlie was dead, it would be him.

Looking completely undeterred at finding a dead

body hanging in the gym, Ice walked over and placed a hand on Charlie's neck.

"The good news is he is very much dead," Ice said slowly. "Too long ago to try to revive him if we were inclined to do so."

"The bad news?" Mannix was stepping around the gym, looking for any more surprises.

"He's still slightly warm," Ice said. "If I had to guess, I'd say he died about an hour ago. Without a thermometer, I can't be certain, but close enough."

"What is he even doing here?" Ares narrowed his eyes as though Charlie was still some kind of threat. He turned those accusing, blue eyes on me. "Didn't you fire his ass?"

"I very much fired his ass," I agreed. "As to what he's doing here, your guess is as good as mine. Wild guess though, it's a message for me, from my dear father."

Asshole.

"What a shame." Ice sighed. "I was looking forward to getting my hands on him myself. I would have already, but we got busy with other things." He shot Mannix a frown for some reason.

"I'm sorry you missed out on your fun," I said sarcastically. "Is there any chance you can remove him from my silk?" I was going to have to have that pulled down and washed. Or better yet, burnt. I couldn't use it now. Or teach children to use an apparatus that was used to strangle someone.

"Sure." Ice unwound the polyester fabric from Charlie's throat and let him flop onto the mat like a heavy doll.

Charlie lay there looking roughly in my direction, eyes still open as though accusing me of having something to do with this.

"He brought it on himself." Ares stepped out from the back of the gym. "Somebody broke the lock in the back door to gain entry. My guess is Charlie. Somebody stumbled upon him and ended him."

He seemed satisfied with that conclusion. He certainly wasn't going to shed any tears over Charlie's death.

Neither was I, but it was as disturbing as hell. Of all the things I expected to find here today, a dead former employee wasn't one of them. Thank goodness it wasn't one of the kids. The thought made my stomach turn.

"It could have been Bell's people breaking in and bringing him with them?" I suggested.

"They would have picked the lock," Mannix said. "Or waited until you unlocked the place. Breaking and entering is too petty a crime for people like them and us. We only resort to it when we have to."

"Or we pay someone else to do it," Ice said. "But I tend to agree. More than one person found him here and killed him. Otherwise things would be in disarray and his skin would be bruised. He barely even has a hair out of place."

"Wonderful." I sat down on one of the padded boxes we used for vaulting and other things. "So Charlie broke in for what? Revenge? Money? To steal a few gym mats? And at least two more were trying to break in, but killed him instead?"

None of this made any sense. As far as I could tell, most of the people in Dusk Bay loved Charlie. He was very good at putting on a façade of being a nice guy. Everyone's best friend. The perfect gymnastics coach. Until he was handcuffing you to a chair and calling up the people you're running from to tell them where you are. Lucky for me that turned out okay.

Unlucky for him, it seemed.

I pinched my nose and sat thinking for a couple of minutes, trying to get my head around all of this. Trying, but failing.

Finally, I got up and walked over to the office. I peered through the window which separated the office from the rest of the gym. All I saw was darkness, apart from a light on the charger to indicate the computer was fully charged.

The door, worn from years of use, was closed. The white paint on its surface was faded, chipped and scratched here and there. Much of the surface was dotted with old pieces of sticky tape, some with scraps of paper still attached. At chest height, was a piece of A3 paper with a grid of all the classes, their times and the students' names. Several names were crossed out as children left, and a few more were added in blue pen underneath the printed lists.

I made a note to print out a new one. This one was looking messy. Maybe when the new term began.

I tried the handle. It was still locked. I pulled out the key, unlocked it and opened the door. It swung into the office with no effort or sound.

My gaze scanned the room and I frowned. "It doesn't look like anything was taken. Or even touched. Unless they locked up behind themselves."

"Step out of there," Mannix said, his body as stiff as his tone.

His anxiety was immediately contagious. I was already as on edge as fuck, but his urging made it worse.

"Why? What are you—"

He cut me off. "Princess, step out of the fucking office. *Now*."

I shrugged, but did as he ordered. "Fine, but I don't see—"

He kept his eyes on the office, but responded to me. "Let us see. You said it yourself, they might have locked up behind themselves."

My blood froze.

CHAPTER ELEVEN

KENNEDY

"You think someone planted a bomb in there?" I looked back through the office door and squinted, as though one might suddenly jump out at us and shout, "Boo." Or, you know, explode.

"I think it's possible." Mannix's gaze swept across all of us. He was obviously wondering if he should tell us to get out of the building while he searched.

"They might be waiting for us outside," Ares said, narrowed eyes looking toward the street.

Mannix nodded. "Stay there." Without further hesitation, he hurried into the office and closed the door behind him. Neither the glass nor the door would be much protection against a bomb, but that was Mannix. He'd always do what he could to protect the people he loved.

Ice pulled his phone out of his back pocket and tapped on the screen.

"What are you doing?" Ares eyed him doubtfully.

"I thought I'd put on some suspenseful music." Ice glanced up and grinned at him.

"How about you fucking don't?" Ares growled. He raised a hand like he was about to knock Ice's phone out of his hand.

Ice swivelled his upper body to keep the phone out of Ares's reach. He tapped the screen and the theme song from the movie franchise *Jaws* sounded out of the phone's speaker.

"You're an idiot," Ares told him.

I flopped back onto the block I vacated a couple of minutes earlier and wondered why this was my life now. I was in my gym with one guy searching for a bomb, another guy playing crazy music, while another was pissed off and forth one was dead.

How had I even come to be in this place?

"Should we have left Charlie how he was and contacted the police?" I asked.

"I've already texted to have someone come clean him up," Ares said. He was watching Ice. The moment the other guy got close enough, he snatched his phone out of his hand and mashed his finger on the screen.

The music didn't stop playing.

"If you don't turn this fucking phone off, I'm going to shoot the shit out of it." He threw it at Ice's chest.

Ice caught it and pressed on the screen until the phone was silent. "Spoilsport. I could start humming."

"Only if you want me to shoot the shit out of you," Ares growled. He stalked over to the back door and stood waiting, presumably for the cleanup crew.

"I always thought his problem was that he needed to get laid," Ice said thoughtfully. "Evidently it runs much deeper than that."

"Fuck off," Ares called out. "Maybe the problem is that I have to put up with you."

Ice cocked his head like a puppy. "I guess that's possible, but I've never found myself that difficult to tolerate."

"You're very tolerable," I assured him. "Better than tolerable."

He moved over to sit beside me and draped his arm over my shoulders.

"This might not be the time to tell you, what with potentially being blown up or whatever, but in case we don't get another chance I thought you should know." He looked at me softly and smiled. "Kennedy Knight-Bell, I love you."

My heart skipped a handful of beats like a routine full of cartwheels.

"Isaac 'Iceman' Miller, I love you too. But if you call me Knight-Bell again, I might let Ares shoot you," I said sweetly.

He chuckled. "It's so hot when you're a badass. Which is most of the time. In fact, I'm so turned on right now, I'd happily fuck you over this box." He tapped his other hand on the padded surface beside him.

"Even with Charlie staring at us with dead eyes?" I jerked my head in his direction, but didn't look.

"Especially then," Ice agreed. "I've never been into necrophilia, but fucking in front of corpses has always had a particular place in my heart. Not as much as when they're still alive though."

He really was a couple of nuts short of the tree, but I adored him for it. Life was too short not to roll with it the way he did. Well, maybe not exactly the way he did, but with a positive approach to things.

We both turned and started to stand at the sound of voices from the back door. After a moment, I realised it was a couple of men in dark coveralls. The cleanup crew. Ares had let them in.

They hurried in, barely acknowledged my existence before they scooped up Charlie and hurried back out with him carried between them.

"What are they going to do with him?" I asked. "People are going to know he disappeared. As soon as they do that, they'll ask questions." I had no idea what to say if they asked me.

"They'll figure out something that will make it look like an accident," Ice said. "No one will be asking or answering any questions about him. His family will get closure, and no one will look twice in the direction of any of us. Which is fair enough, because we actually didn't do anything this time." He scratched the side of his head and shrugged.

"Yeah, I guess we didn't," I agreed. "When Mannix is done in the office, I can check the video feed and see if it caught anything."

We had the same doubtful expression on our faces. If whoever killed Charlie had the skills to pick a lock, they would have disabled the security cameras.

"Why didn't Charlie trip the security alarm?" I asked. I forgot it existed until now. I wasn't used to living my life with measures like that.

"It must have been disabled before he broke in," Ice said thoughtfully.

Thoughts tumbled around in my head and it took a moment to make them coherent.

"So...it's possible they were watching. Turned off the alarm, let him get into the place, then followed him and killed him?"

"Or turned it off, meaning to let themselves in, but he happened to turn up at the same time. Or he saw them and followed. He might have been trying to stop them." Ice turned his phone around in his hands.

That suggestion made my blood run cold again. Was there any possibility Charlie was trying to do the right thing? He might have been trying to protect the place to be nice or in the hope of getting his job back.

I might have considered hiring him again, but that was out of the question now. The animosity between us when we saw each other last would stand between us forever, no chance to make amends.

Would we have made up, given more time? That was moot, because we couldn't anyway.

"You said the people that killed him were unlikely to be the ones who broke the lock," I pointed out. "Unless they're trying to pin that on Charlie. We're never going to know are we? They would have turned off the cameras so no one could see what they did."

For some reason, that made me feel more violated than ever. It was bad enough that people were running around in my gym killing people, but they were covering their tracks and leaving us firmly in the dark.

Except for one thing. Samuel Bell was behind all of this. Perhaps not Charlie breaking in, but the rest of it. If Charlie had been trying to help, he was dead because of me. My hands might as well have been coated in his blood.

"Sometimes getting the answer doesn't matter," Ice said. "Either way, Charlie was somewhere he shouldn't have been and he's dead because of it. It's unlikely to be the end of whatever this is. Even if there isn't a bomb, there's a reason for everything. Shit like this doesn't go down at random."

"That's what I'm worried about." I watched the cleanup guys slip out the back door.

I caught a glimpse of them loading Charlie into a van parked on the street behind the gym. They hefted him in like a sack of potatoes and slammed the doors shut behind him. They climbed into the van and were gone like they were never here.

Like Charlie never existed at all.

I sighed. We had our disagreements, but he wasn't the worst person in the world. Not even the second worst.

"The kids are going to be devastated," I said softly. Just because he wasn't their coach anymore didn't mean they didn't adore him. People like him played a big part in kid's lives. Their first somersault. First handstand. First cartwheel. For many it was a chance to discover a sport they enjoyed. For others it was just a few hours of fun.

Either way, Charlie was the centre of a lot of it and now he was gone.

It wasn't that long ago I'd never seen a dead body. Now I'd seen more than I could count. I'd come close to becoming one myself. Was this my life now? Death everywhere? Would I get used to it at some point? Did I want to? Were the guys worth all of this?

"They'll get over it," Ice said. "After all, they still have you."

"Unless we get blown up." I pressed the palms of my hands to the block and levered myself higher to peer into the office. Every so often, Mannix's head bobbed up and down as he crouched and stood and crouched again.

"Unless that," Ice agreed. "I might go and see how

Mannix is doing in there. Stay here." Before I could argue, he jumped off the box and strode over to the office.

Hating to sit idly by, I stood and walked over to the silk beside the one which was used to strangle Charlie. I gripped the fabric in two hands and started to climb.

When I was high enough, I drew up my legs and climbed higher, using a series of knots with my feet to push myself up. My ass hurt, but I pushed the pain aside and kept going.

I reached the ceiling and wound the silk around my wrist a couple of times. I wound my foot under the silk and stood on that foot with the other, locking me in place.

Satisfied I wouldn't fall, I swung a couple of times, until I was close enough to grab the other silk. I pulled myself over closer, tugging until I could reach the heavy clip on top of the silk. It was tight, but I managed to unscrew it and unclip the silk from the hook that fastened it to the ceiling.

I let it go. The silk fell to the floor in a flutter of tainted, polyester fabric.

I watched its passage until it landed in a puddle on the mats below. It looked beautiful and innocent, not like something that was used to murder a man in cold blood.

Was it really necessary to do something like that in a space like this? This was supposed to be where children came to have fun and learn new skills. Not where adult men came to die.

I let go with both hands and held the silk with my thighs as I plummeted towards the floor. A metre off, I stopped myself and grinned at the adrenaline rush. I lowered my palms to the mat and did a somersault, letting go of the silks at the last moment. I landed on my feet and dropped my hands to my sides.

"That was fucking hot," Ares declared. He looked impressed.

I smiled and gave him a curtsy. "The silks are my happy place."

"Me too," he agreed. "Silk sheets." His gaze slid up and down my body.

I laughed, but it died away when Mannix stepped out of the office, a grim expression on his face.

CHAPTER TWELVE

KENNEDY

Mannix rubbed the back of his head. "I didn't find anything that looked like a bomb. It doesn't look like anything in there was touched." He glanced over his shoulder like he was sure he missed something, but knew he hadn't. He'd searched thoroughly. If there was anything to find, he would have found it.

Ice cocked his head at Mannix. "So, no bomb?"

"No bomb," Mannix agreed. "That doesn't rule out a virus on the computer. I wouldn't put it past them to use our tactic against us. But..." He frowned and shook his head. "If they were going to do that, they'd go after someone higher up than us. Attacking us like that they wouldn't achieve very much. Bell is an asshole, but petty revenge isn't usually his style."

"There's only one way to find out." I took a step towards the office, but Mannix grabbed my arm.

"It can wait." Something in his tone made me stop and look at him.

"You're going to need a new one of those." He nodded toward the silk that lay on the mat.

"Yeah, I'm going to have to order one." I wrinkled my nose.

"Yes, you are, because we're going to make that very one sticky."

He hooked his fingers into the front of my shorts and pulled me to him. Before I could protest, he had them undone. He shoved them and my panties down my thighs.

They fell to my feet, leaving the bottom half of me bare.

"I don't know if this is a good idea." I still stepped out of them. I knew that expression on his face all too well. He wasn't asking.

"It's not a good idea," he agreed. "It's a great idea. It's Sunday. No kids are coming. The only ones who are coming are us."

He nodded to the other guys. Between them, Ares and Ice pulled off my shirt and bra.

They lay me down on my back on the fallen silk. It smelled of sweat, cleaning detergent and last gasps.

Charlie dying tangled in the fabric was precisely the point. Mannix and the others were turned on knowing his body dangled there. Knowing he took his last breath amongst the folds of blue polyester.

That was both twisted as fuck and hot as hell at the same time.

I glanced toward the door. We'd left it unlocked.

A row of blocks stood between us and the large glass windows at the front of the gym. If anyone walked past, chances are they wouldn't see us. If they didn't try the door, then no one but us would ever know.

Mannix bent my knees and parted my thighs with his hands. He gave me an intense look before he lowered his mouth to my pussy and licked me from front to back.

I shivered. His touch was unusually feather light, but it drove me wild even faster than when he was rough and merciless. From the look in his eyes, he knew it too.

Ice sat beside me, his legs tucked underneath him. He looked at me like I was a sculpture, a work of art for him to appreciate.

He pulled out his phone and gave me a questioning look.

I hesitated, but eventually nodded. I trusted him

not to share with anyone but Mannix and Ares. Of course he wouldn't. If anyone else saw me naked, Ice would poke their eyes out.

He smiled, held up his phone and took a couple of photos of me, Mannix's face between my legs.

"Something for later." He put his phone away, leaned forward and went to work on my nipples. Licking and sucking like they were the sweetest treat he ever had.

Ares undid his shorts and lay beside me, his cock in front of my face. He really was huge.

"You could put out someone's eye with that thing." I closed one of mine and looked at him appreciatively.

Ares chuckled. "Open up," he said. "I'm going to fuck your mouth."

I opened my mouth and he pressed the tip of his cock between my lips. He was so big, I wasn't sure how much I could take.

"Good girl. You can take more." He pushed in deeper, all the way to the back of my throat. "There you go, I knew you could take me." He grabbed my hand and placed it on his balls.

I massaged and sucked as Mannix nipped and teased my clit.

Pleasure curled through my body, starting at my

core and expanding from there like a slow growing vine. It grew faster when he slipped his fingers inside me and fucked me with his hand and his tongue.

My orgasm exploded like a supernova, burning hot enough to incinerate me and everything around me. I took my mouth off Ares's cock long enough to breathe while I shattered.

My whole body was deliciously on fire. I arched my back and rocked against his face, coating his mouth and hand with my juices.

I shouted Mannix's name to the ceiling. And again when I came for a second time.

By the time I came down, my head was spinning, but my body throbbed for more.

Mannix raised his face and smiled. "I want you both to taste how she tastes when she comes."

He moved up beside me, stopping to kiss Ice before he reached me. His tongue swept over my lips, sliding inside and spreading my flavour.

Ice smacked his lips. "Delicious. If I could bottle the way you two taste together, I'd be rich. Okay, richer."

I wasn't sure anyone would buy something like that, but people bought all sorts of interesting things, so why not my juices?

I licked my lips. Not bad.

The taste of myself on my lips, I went back to spoiling Ares' cock.

"Did you bring what I told you to bring?" Mannix asked Ice as he started to shed his clothes.

I watched from the corner of my eye without stopping sucking and licking. Ares groaned in pleasure. I loved the sounds he made. They were pure magic. Pure, hot magic.

Ice frowned at him for a moment, then realised what Mannix was referring to. "Right." He patted his pockets. "Phone. Gun. Ahhh... Here we go. Lube." He pulled out a small tube and tossed it to Mannix.

Mannix caught it. "Strip."

Ice did so without hesitation.

"Fuck her." He nodded towards me.

"Gladly." Ice smiled at me.

I smiled back with my eyes, my mouth being busy and full of cock. I wanted him inside me right now. My pussy ached to be filled. I bent my knees and parted my thighs for him.

"Beautiful." Ice knelt between my knees and positioned his cock before he slid the entirety of his length deep inside me.

I sighed with pleasure at being filled. Nothing in the world felt quite like it.

"Lean forward," Mannix told Ice. He squeezed

lube onto his fingers and moved around behind the other guy.

I watched Ice's expression as Mannix prepared his rear hole. I couldn't see, but I could imagine, and what I pictured was pretty fucking hot.

"Ready." It was a statement, not a question. Mannix gripped Ice's hips and moved his own hips forward.

Ice's eyes widened. Mannix was sliding inside him.

Holy shit.

The movement pushed Ice deeper inside me. I groaned around Ares' cock.

Mannix stopped to let Ice get used to him, then started to move, slow and careful.

All three guys pumped and ground in rhythm, deeper and harder into me, driving me closer and closer to the edge of blissful oblivion.

I took my mouth off Ares again and worked him with my hand while I came. This time was longer, but somehow softer than the other two. Floating on a cloud rather than being in the centre of a tornado. The bliss went on for days, gently pushing every other thought or feeling aside until that was all that existed.

When it drifted away, finally, I sighed.

"Fuck, that's always hot. Open back up."

Ares just managed to slip his cock back between my lips in time for his own orgasm. He thrust hard a couple of times, eyes scrunched closed in concentration and ecstasy.

He grunted and tangled his fingers in my hair. He tugged hard as his body stilled.

"Fuck yeah."

Hot cum squirted from his tip, flooding my mouth and down my throat. I sucked harder, wanting every drop from him. Every last bit.

Finally he sagged, panting out his nose, his face tinged pink. He slipped his cock out of my mouth and fixed his blue eyes on me.

"Swallow it." He watched me like he wasn't sure I'd do exactly as he ordered. As if I'd spit in his face, or on the silk.

I swallowed.

He smiled, satisfied, like he got the cream instead of me. "You're so fucking hot." He leaned down to kiss me, his tongue swiping over my lips and plunging inside.

He fucked my mouth with his tongue as Ice fucked my body.

As Mannix fucked his.

"Fuck, you feel so good," Mannix panted. "So tight."

Ice grunted something that could have been an agreement. "I'm going to come inside you, Beautiful."

"I was going to say that," Mannix said with a small laugh. Right before he came. His eyes half closed, mouth half open, the same blissed out expression Ares had on his face a couple of minutes earlier.

"Fucking hell, you're so...ahhh. Holy fuck..."

Ice followed a moment later, thrusting into me and moaning so loud I couldn't stop myself from coming for a fourth time.

This one was longer, but so powerful it rocked my entire body, down to the roots of my hair, my toenails, my fingertips.

We all flopped down, panting. Every bit as sticky as Mannix promised.

I was definitely going to need a new silk now, because this one was ruined.

CHAPTER THIRTEEN

KENNEDY

"Shit."

Mannix's sudden exclamation made me pause, my finger on the button to open the gate.

"What is it?" I was feeling more relaxed after our group fuck, but the single word put me right back on edge.

"Open the gate and don't panic." He nodded towards my hand and waited until the gate was open wide enough to drive the SUV through. In other words, with half a hair between the car and the gates.

How he made it through every time, I didn't know. I would have scraped half the paint off if I tried.

"You realise the words most likely to make me panic are, 'don't panic,' right?" I asked.

A couple of dark cars were parked to the side of the driveway. They could suggest any number of things. Most of them one hundred percent not good.

Mannix didn't smile in response. He pulled the SUV into the garage and waved us all toward the door that led into the house.

All three guys wore the same, intense expression on their faces. They were definitely expecting something bad. Not so bad we turned tail and ran, but bad nonetheless.

I stopped in front of the door and raised my hands, positioning myself so no one could open it.

"Would someone please explain what's going on?" I lowered my hands to my hips and looked from one to the other. "I'm not going inside until I get some answers."

I narrowed my eyes at them, for added effect.

"Chances are my brother is here," Mannix said finally and reluctantly. Apparently my attempted intimidation worked. Go me. "With Daze, Ric and Hilton."

"Okay," I said slowly. "I'm guessing this isn't a family catch-up?"

Instead of answering, he put his hands on my shoulders and moved me aside. Keeping one hand on my shoulder, he steered me through the doorway.

We followed voices to the formal living room to the side of the house.

"Here they are." Mum greeted me as though we were supposed to be home hours ago. Her expression matched Mannix's.

Leo stood beside her, guarded, his body stiff.

Daisy Lasalle, or Daze as she was known, sat on the long white couch, Ric DiMarco on one side, Mannix's brother Gunnar on the other. Her third boyfriend, Hilton Blake, sat in an armchair beside her, legs crossed at his knees.

I glanced at her and smiled. She smiled back reassuringly, but both of our gazes soon slid to the other two men in the room.

If I wanted to ignore them, I couldn't have. Their presence made the air heavier, like a massive thundercloud, heavy with promise of destruction.

"This is Caleb Brantley," Leo said, his tone lighter than his expression.

Caleb regarded me with dark, dangerous eyes.

I could have guessed who he was just by looking at him. The resemblance between him, Hunter and Parker, and Zeke Brantley was obvious. He wore a perfectly tailored suit and dark tie. Everything about him screamed money and ruthless power.

"And Mack D'Antonio." Leo nodded to the

other man. He was equally well dressed and dangerous looking. A handkerchief peeked out of his suit pocket, matching the piercing blue of his eyes. The kind that could eviscerate a soul with a glance.

"Hey." I tried to smile but the way everyone was looking at me made me want to pee myself.

Caleb looked me up and down like I was a slab of beef in the butcher shop and he wasn't sure he liked what he saw.

Mack seemed unimpressed. He carried the air that he'd pull out a gun and use it without a second thought. He'd be hot if he wasn't kinda scary at the same time.

"It's good to see you again." Daze put her coffee aside and stood to give me a hug. "Leo tells us you've had quite a surprise about your parentage. I wanted to come and see you. Everyone else came along out of curiosity. Don't worry about them, they won't bite you. I won't let them."

She gave *all* the men in the room a narrow-eyed look, including Leo and my guys.

"You don't have the authority here," Caleb said, his voice both soft and cold.

I could have gone skiing on his tone.

Daze didn't back down. "Maybe not, but I won't

let a young woman be hurt just because of who her father is."

"If any harm comes to Ms Knight, it won't be because of that," Caleb said. "Her parentage is irrelevant. I'm more concerned with her behaviour."

My behaviour?

I would have moved over closer to my guys, but there was no need. They stepped around me like a wall of hot muscle.

"Kennedy has done nothing out of line." Mannix's tone was as cold as Caleb. "She risked her life to help try to take down Samuel Bell."

"Tried and failed," Caleb pointed out.

"But still tried." Mannix wasn't giving a centimetre.

"My daughter has done nothing wrong," Mum argued.

Caleb turned his cold, dark eyes to her. "Your failure to mention her paternity also makes you suspect."

She actually took a step back from him. It was the first time in my life I ever saw my mother truly scared.

Her tongue darted over her lips. "I was trying to protect my child. I wanted her to have a better, safer life than she would have had if he knew about her."

Caleb was perfectly illustrating why she wasn't forthcoming. If this was the reaction, maybe I was better off never knowing.

That cat was firmly out of the bag. How did Caleb know? I doubted I needed to look much past Leo. These were the kind of things a dutiful minion didn't keep from their boss. If I ended up under a bus, it was because he threw me there.

"I have no intention of having anything to do with him." I tilted my chin and met Caleb's eyes. Somehow I managed to sound like my knees weren't shaking. This man held my life in his hands. He could end it with a nod.

And then the guys would go to war with him. One they couldn't win. Caleb had the numbers on his side in this room alone. One look and all of our blood would stain the carpet.

Oh goodie.

"My loyalty is here." I didn't mean him specifically, but if that was how he interpreted it, then fine. It wouldn't hurt if he believed that. It was close enough to the truth. My guys were loyal to him and I was loyal to them. By extension, what I said was accurate.

I considered reminding Caleb his twin brothers'

loyalty might be more suspect than mine, but decided that was a can of worms I was better off not touching, much less opening.

Caleb seemed angry enough as it was. He was the second oldest Brantley brother. I wondered if Reuben was scarier than him. If he was, I didn't want to meet him.

Caleb was more than enough.

And Mack. What was his role in all of this? There was a passing resemblance between him and Hilton, along with the same dark intensity. But then, all of the guys in the room had that.

It was like a testosterone factory in here. Or an alpha male convention.

Caleb stared me down.

I almost looked away.

Before I did, he said, "Be sure it is. Those three boys have given us enough trouble going off on their own. Don't let them drag you down with them." The message was obvious. Don't drag them down either.

I had no intention of that. Although, where could I possibly lead them that they wouldn't go on their own, or wouldn't be sent by someone like Caleb Brantley?

I reminded myself I was only starting to learn

about this life. What little I knew was probably the tip of a big, dangerous iceberg, so to speak. One with possibilities I couldn't even imagine right now.

"My understanding was that the virus idea was Kennedy's," Ric said. "It seems she's well on her way to leading those three astray."

Gunnar grunted his agreement. "It's not like my brother needs much help, but if he was going to fuck up, it would be because of a pretty face."

"Pretty faces have a way of doing that," Hilton said. He turned a smile on Daze.

She smiled warmly back at him.

"A tight pussy is the root of all evil," Ric remarked.

Daze rolled her eyes playfully. "Men have been thinking with their cocks since the dawn of time. And blaming women for it."

Mack rolled his eyes.

"I don't think Mack agrees with you," Ric said.

"Men and women have both been thinking with their genitals since humans began," Mack said, his voice cold whiskey over ice. "That's never changed and it never will."

I hadn't noticed a network of scars down the side of his face until now. What would have caused those? They looked old, like he got them when he was my age. Were they from a reckless youth, or something more?

I wouldn't put it past anyone in this room to do dangerous things that resulted in scars, including myself.

"Why did the virus fail?" Caleb asked suddenly.

I turned my gaze back to him. "He anticipated something like that being sent at him at some point," I said. "I didn't, *couldn't,* account for that. There was no way to know how he had things set up."

"Unless you went there ahead of time," he said.

"Unless that," I agreed. "There was no way to do that though, or to know that we needed to."

"You should have anticipated." His gaze burned into my soul.

"Maybe, but I'm new to this." I wasn't backing down. He could point all the fingers he wanted, we did the best we could with the information we had.

I could blame the people who got that information in the first place, but that didn't seem productive. Also, since they worked for him, he was probably well aware of the shortcomings. If he'd come here looking for a scapegoat, he'd have to keep looking. I wasn't putting my hand up for that role.

He turned his eyes towards the guys. "You're not new to this. Not as new as she is."

Mannix shrugged. "We knew what we knew and we did the best we could with that. We gave Bell a fright and got out of there alive. And we took at least a dozen of his people down."

Surely that counted for something?

Caleb turned back to me. "Did he give you any indication he'd welcome interaction with you?"

I blinked in nervous surprise. "He didn't exactly send me an invitation to Christmas lunch, if that's what you mean. I haven't been inundated by twenty-one years of back-birthday and Christmas presents."

Yet.

"But he didn't tell you to stay away?" Caleb asked.

I glanced at the guys, then told him about Charlie.

Mum gasped in horror, but no one else seemed all that surprised or concerned.

"Unless it had something to do with you, then it's possible my fa— Bell had people kill Charlie in my gym," I concluded.

Caleb nodded slowly. "If that's the case, he'll contact you at some point. I want you to keep me posted."

"No," Mannix said.

All eyes turned to him. "If you're thinking of sending her as some kind of double agent, to work against Bell in his house, then no fucking way. I am not risking her like that." He gave Caleb a death stare.

Caleb responded with indifference. "If I send her, that's where she'll go. This isn't a debate or a democracy. If I give an order, you'll follow it. I don't give a shit if you like it or not."

He didn't even have to raise his voice, his tone insisted on obedience. Since the alternative was probably a horrible, painful death, no doubt he got it more often than not.

Mannix growled in the back of his throat, deep but soft. "If you send her—"

I grabbed his arm before he could do or say anything he'd regret. "He wouldn't send me if it wasn't safe, but I doubt Bell is going to contact me and extend an invitation. Don't argue over nothing."

I thought he was going to shake me off, but instead he exhaled loudly and took a step back. "Fine, but if anything happens to you because of him—"

"Nothing will happen to me. You're here to make sure of that. Whatever happens, I'll be fine. Okay?" I locked stern eyes on his stubborn ones.

He gave a short nod. "I need coffee. Let's get out of here."

I glanced at Caleb long enough to see him jerk his head towards the door, giving us permission to leave his presence.

I couldn't get out of there fast enough.

CHAPTER FOURTEEN

KENNEDY

Mannix and Ares took turns pacing across the room.

Ice and I lay on Mannix's bed, thighs pressed together. His nose was buried in my hair. He slowly wound tendrils around his fingers. My eyes were half closed as I tried not to drift off to sleep.

"Can you believe that asshole?" Mannix growled. It was his turn to pace, while Ares leaned against the wall and watched him. "He actually suggested sending Kennedy back to Bell. As if we'd fucking let that happen."

"If he makes her go, we can't stop him." Ares didn't seem to like the words he was speaking any more than Mannix did.

"The hell we can't," Mannix snapped. He stalked over to the window and back again.

"What are you going to do? Go to war against the whole Brantley family? Bro, we're no use to anyone if we're dead." Ares' customary scowl was back in place.

"I'd rather be dead than let Kennedy go back there," Mannix said.

"If you're dead, he's going to send her back anyway," Ares pointed out.

Mannix rounded on him, but couldn't deny the truth of what he said.

"He might not be planning to do that," Ice said without lifting his face to look at them. He inhaled like he was breathing in the scent of me. As if I was some exotic perfume, or drug.

"I hope he's not," I said sleepily. If I ended up back in the basement room, I doubted anyone would let me go a second time. How long would it take to die down there? Not long once I gave up on the idea of ever getting out again.

I shuddered.

"You okay, Beautiful?" Ice asked. His eyes peered through a wall of my hair like he was looking through a hedge.

"Yeah, just remembering the basement."

To my surprise, Ares walked over and slumped

down beside me. I hadn't seen him look worried before, but he did now.

"It's okay to be affected by shit like that. That kind of sensory and sleep deprivation is designed to fuck with people. It's literally one of the worst forms of torture known to humans."

Right, he studied psychology. If anyone knew about stuff like that, it was him.

I smiled faintly. "Is, 'shit like that,' the clinical term?"

"In my clinic it is." He cocked his head. "You want to talk about it?"

"You should," Ice said. "It'll make you feel better."

He was probably right, but I didn't know what to say.

I squeezed Ice's hand when he curled his fingers around mine.

"It was a whole bunch of nothing," I said finally. "It felt like I was stuck in a black hole, with nothing but my thoughts."

It wasn't one of those nice, relaxing sensory deprivation tanks people pay money to lie in for an hour or so. This was hour after hour in a cold, dark space.

"Places like that can cause hallucinations," Ares

said. "The brain can do strange things when it has nothing else to do."

"Are you saying this is a hallucination?" I poked him on the arm with my fingernail. "You feel real."

"That's because I am real." He grabbed my hand and brought it to his mouth.

I thought he'd kiss it. Instead, he placed my pointer finger between his lips and sucked gently.

Fuck, that was hot.

"I might not be real," Ice said dreamily. "Sometimes I feel like I'm not. I might be real and I might not be here at all."

"You're not all here," Ares agreed.

"I've heard sanity is overrated anyway." Ice smiled.

"Who told you that?" I asked.

"Not me," Mannix said from the other side of the room. "We're all a little bit out of our minds here."

"Speak for yourself." Ares shot him a look.

"I was." Mannix shrugged. "If you're the only sane one around here, then the rest of us are fucked."

"There's nothing wrong with being fucked," Ice said. "In fact, it's one of my favourite things."

"Unless we're being fucked *over*." Mannix, who seemed to have forgotten for a moment how pissed off he was, resumed pacing. "Then it's not fucking okay."

"Would Caleb send me back to Bell if it wasn't for some specific purpose?" I asked.

"He might ask you to spy on Bell for the rest of your life," Ares said. He also looked pissed off again. "Which wouldn't be very long if you got caught. Or even if he suspected that's why you were there."

There was a big difference between proclaiming my loyalty to the Brantley family and being asked to do something like that. Especially for a long period of time.

"Do they know the twins are seeing Lila?" Bell was clearly not happy about it, but what would Caleb think?

"Either they don't know, or they sent the twins in to seduce her." Mannix shrugged indifferently. "I don't know and I'm not gonna ask. That shit is well above my pay grade."

I grimaced. "Is that something that happens often? Guys sent to seduce women? Or the other way around?" If they did that to me, I'd be gutted. Imagine falling for someone only to find out it was all an act. A pretence to find information, or to get to you in some way.

"Maybe not often, but it happens," Ares said.

"I heard a rumour that Reuben sent one of his younger brothers, Lucas, to seduce some woman from a rival family." Mannix curled his lip in disgust. "Last I heard, she was pregnant."

I gaped at him while my stomach turned. "That's horrible. Would any of you do anything like that?"

"Not to you," Ice said immediately. "For the record, I've never been asked to do something like that."

"Me either," Mannix said.

"Neither have I, and I wouldn't," Ares said. "Fuck that. I'm not a whore." He pointed a warning finger at Ice, who looked like he was about to joke or contradict him. "Don't say a word or I'll rip your tongue out."

Ice raised a hand in surrender.

"My mother didn't know the Brantley family until after she was with Samuel Bell, right?" I said slowly.

They all looked at me.

"That was what she said," Mannix said. He pressed his lips together. "You think she was sent to seduce him and ended up getting pregnant?"

"I'm prepared to believe just about anything right now." I sighed and sank back deeper against the pillow. "What about that Mack guy? Who is he and where does he fit into all of this?"

"He's hot, isn't he?" Ice's sigh came on the tail of mine.

Mannix cut him a warning look.

"Just looking, not gonna touch," Ice said lightly.

"You better not, because if I have to kill him for touching you, that's gonna create a shit storm." Mannix crossed his arms. "Mack D'Antonio is a friend of Caleb. As much as Caleb has any friends. He's also got more money than Caleb, Reuben, and Bell combined. He's involved in mining or some shit."

"Legal stuff?" I asked.

Ares said, "Some of it's legal, some of it isn't. He does a lot of business here in Dusk Bay. He has a house on the other side of the city, on the promontory. It's about twice the size of this one. He's only there a couple of times of year."

"What a waste." I wrinkled my nose.

"He can afford it," Mannix said.

"Lifestyles of the famous and obscenely rich," I said. It was slightly sickening.

"Obscenely rich is an accurate definition for it," Ice said. "But they still bleed the same."

"Tortured any billionaires lately, have you?" Ares teased.

"Not recently and not nearly often enough." Ice let out an exaggerated sigh. "For what it's worth, sometimes I pretend they're someone other than who they are. That gets me by pretty well."

"If I get my hands on Samuel Bell, he's all yours," Mannix promised. "Just save a little bit for all of us."

"Especially me." I couldn't get the idea of my mother being sent to seduce him out of my head. I considered the possibility it was the other way around, but for what purpose? My mother was no one significant in the scheme of things. Not when it came to the power-play between all these families. As far as I knew anyway.

I'd established by now that the more I learnt, the more I realised I didn't know. She could be a queen in exile, or fuck knows what else.

I shook my head at the thought.

"What do you need to get into Brutham Academy?" I asked.

"Are you thinking of going?" Ice curled a section of my hair around his finger and let it bounce free before curling it again.

"No, I was wondering how and why my mother went there."

Ice's hand stilled. "Most students have to be nominated by their family. Or by one of the more powerful families. If someone works for Caleb Brantley, for example, he could nominate their children to go. Of course, they'd be expected to work for him after they finished their degree."

"Leo nominated me," Ares said softly.

"Me too." Ice went back to playing with my hair. "Only Mannix got in directly."

"My mother must have had ties to the Brantleys long before I was born," I reasoned.

"In some capacity, she must have," Ice agreed.

I didn't want to believe she seduced Bell because she was told to. The idea of her having feelings for him was icky, but it was better than thinking I was an unfortunate accident. A pregnancy that resulted from some kind of power-play.

I couldn't even begin to imagine what that might have involved. A distraction? Some effort to get Samuel Bell on their side? Or maybe the Bell family wanted my mother on their side?

All of this was starting to give me a massive headache.

"I know it matters to you how you came about," Ares said, his tone low and soft, unusually sensitive. "But it doesn't matter to us. We don't care who fucked whom and why. What matters is that you're you and you're ours. All of that shit happened a long time ago. It doesn't change anything."

There was no hint of hesitation or reservation in his voice or on his face. Every single word he said was one hundred percent sincere. If he ever really hated me, he'd put it firmly behind him.

I managed a watery smile. "Thank you. That means a lot. I thought you all might walk away when you knew who my father was." I frowned. "That's not true. I thought you'd kill me. Daughter of the enemy and all that."

"Nothing you could do or be would make us kill you," Mannix said. "You belong to us. End of story. That's how things are going to stay until the end of time. You're stuck with us until we're all old and grey."

He didn't have to add that it was only applicable if we lived that long. We all knew there was a good chance we wouldn't. Charlie's death brought that home better than anything else could have. Then Caleb looking at me like I was some kind of tool to be used however he wanted...

I might end up pushed and pulled between the Bells and the Brantleys and the guys, or I might end up dead. None of that was ideal. Especially the last one. I wasn't ready to be used as a pawn, but I was even less ready to be swept off the board and onto the floor.

"You're stuck with me until you're old and grey too," I told them. "Which will be sooner, because you're older than me and I intend to keep colouring my hair for as long as I can." I grinned.

"And such pretty hair it is too." Ice gripped a bunch of it in his fist and brought it to his mouth to kiss. "I wonder how I'd look with hair that colour."

"Silly," Ares told him. "Just like I would."

"I think he'd look cute," Mannix said. "We could call him Little Red Riding Cock."

"That's Big Red Riding Cock to you." Ice sniffed.

"Yes it—"

We all jumped when my phone rang.

CHAPTER FIFTEEN

KENNEDY

I leaned over, away from Ice and grabbed my phone off the table beside the bed.

"I don't know the number."

"All in favour of you not answering the phone." Ice raised his hand.

We all looked at Mannix, who was thinking quickly.

"Answer it," he said finally.

"But—"

He cut Ice off. "Answer it. It might be nothing. If it isn't, I want to know about it. Put it on speakerphone."

Reluctantly, I did what he said, then pressed the button to answer the call.

"Hello?" I said tentatively. "Who is this?"

"Kennedy." That was all he said, but I recognised Samuel Bell's voice.

"How did you get this number?" I certainly hadn't given it to him and I didn't know anyone who would.

Bell chuckled. "There's nothing I can't get if I want it. Getting your number was a simple matter."

"Let me guess, if I block this number, you'll try on a different one?" I let Ice pull me back to him and slip an arm around me.

"Yes, but that would be tedious. Don't block this number." There was that, 'I expect to be obeyed,' tone again. That was starting to become normal around here.

"What do you want?" I asked coldly.

"Can't I check up on my daughter?" he asked. "You got home safely?"

"I have a feeling you knew I did," I said. "What do you really want?"

"Did you get my present?"

I frowned. Present? What the hell was he—

Realisation dawned.

"Charlie. That was you." What the ever loving fuck?

"In a manner of speaking," he agreed. "I had my people keep an eye on the gym, to make sure you were okay. They caught him trying to break in, so they dealt with him."

"But the security alarm..."

"Switched off, to avoid drawing attention to the place. If that went off, everyone would have come running and everything would be a lot messier. Wouldn't you agree?"

"Oh yeah," I said sarcastically. "I'm sure it could have been worse than a dead body hanging in my gym. From my silk, which I'm sure you know is my favourite apparatus."

"So I'm told." He sounded like he was reading off a computer screen full of information he or someone had gathered all about me. "You started with gymnastics but your favourite apparatus is a circus trick."

"It's better than being a clown," I said flatly.

He chuckled. "I see you got your sense of humour from me."

"Was that what leaving Charlie dangling like that was? A joke? Because it wasn't fucking funny." His face was going to heavily feature in my nightmares for a while. At least the dreams featuring the guys killing that man outside the masked ball had stopped.

Although, thinking about those masks still made my skin tingle and crawl.

"It wasn't a joke," Bell said smoothly. "It was a warning."

"A warning to me to...what? Stay away from you? A warning that you know where I live and work? Did you do it there because you can't reach me here at home?" It was nice to know somewhere was safe from his reach.

"It wasn't a warning for you," he said slowly and clearly as though he needed me to hear and understand his exact words and meaning. "It was a warning *about* you. That anyone who messes with you will have me to answer to."

His words rattled around in my brain for a minute or two, like those carnival throwing games where the ball rolls around and around the tube before it slowly drops into the hole. Then it rolls down another tube before landing in the wrong place. The number beside the one that would have won the thrower a huge plush hippopotamus.

Yeah, it's happened to me a few times before.

I laughed. "You had your people kill Charlie in my gym as a warning for people to stay away from me?"

"Precisely."

"Who? Who are you warning?" I glanced up at

the guys, but they had no more answers than I did judging by the expressions on their faces.

"Your mother, for one," Bell said. "You told her, didn't you? How did she react?"

I knitted my brows. Any harder and I would have made myself a nice, warm scarf.

"She was horrified," I said slowly. "Like any mother would be if their daughter found a dead body at work."

"Not just any mother. One who knows me. I'd wager a million dollars she's already told you I'd have taken you away from her if I'd known about you sooner."

I wouldn't take that bet, because she had.

"What's your point?" I asked.

"My point is, I want her to know I can reach her too. Because of her, we missed out on a lifetime of being together. She's hurt you in ways you can't imagine."

"And yet, the first time we met, you locked me in that room," I said bitterly.

There was a pause, followed by a heavy sigh. "Perhaps not my finest hour."

I snorted. "No shit, Sherlock. For the record, I don't buy this caring father routine you have going on. In fact, I don't think this is about me at all. I think you're pissed off at my mother and want revenge. I was just collateral damage." And I was really, really tempted to hang up. My finger hovered over the phone screen.

"What did she tell you about our past?" he asked.

"What does it matter?" I asked in return.

"What did she tell you?" he insisted.

I closed my eyes and gritted my teeth for a moment, but forced them back open and for my jaw to relax.

"She told me you had a brief fling. That she cared about you but you all graduated and she never saw you again. She said you were supposed to marry...Penelope?"

It was his turn to sound bitter. "I was hoping she'd tell you the truth, because you'd believe it coming from her. Otherwise I would have told you when you were here."

"Spare me if you're going to tell me a bunch of lies," I snapped.

"Not lies. The complete truth. Whether you want to believe it or not is up to you."

I glanced at the guys again. They didn't look even slightly alike, but right now they wore matching sceptical expressions. If that was all we had to go on, we'd look like quadruplets right now.

Ice would find that thought hilarious, but I shoved it out of my mind for now.

"Fine, I'm listening. Tell me what you think your version of the truth is." I was going to need a big pinch of salt, because I doubted a word of it was worth believing.

"You know we met at Brutham Academy?" he started. He continued before I could confirm that I knew that. "She did everything she could to get my attention. At first, I didn't give her much of it. She was gorgeous and all of the boys and a lot of the girls were after her. I thought there was no way she'd be interested in a guy like me. I always had my nose in a book, as they say. The only things I had going for me were my last name and my parents' money. Back then, none of that meant anything to me. I planned to study archaeology and hand the business over to my brother when he was old enough, and finished at the Academy."

He was silent for a beat or two.

"Finally, Helen managed to convince me she really was interested in me. Not my money. Not my name. I fell in love with her. I decided we could have a future together. Get married, have children, live a life away from the violence and crime." He actually sounded sincere.

"We planned to get engaged after we left Brutham. Then I told her about my plans. We argued. Then she admitted her mother was the one who wanted her to go after me. She was a longtime employee of the Brantley family, but she was tired of seeing their wealth and power, while she and her daughter went without. She got Helen into Brutham Academy and set her on the course to change that."

I pictured him sitting at his desk, his eyes closed. Maybe rubbing the bridge of his nose, or his temples. I didn't want to feel sympathy for him. I didn't want to feel anything for him, but he seemed genuine. He also could have been laying a trap I was walking straight into with my soft heartedness.

"So you broke up?" I guessed.

"In a manner of speaking," he said. "I wanted to stay with her regardless of how we started out. My father had other ideas. He decided I should marry Penelope. He offered Helen three million dollars to stay away from me. It was more than Helen would have made being married to an archaeologist, so she took it. I never saw her again. It wasn't until she announced her engagement to Leo that I realised she had a daughter. Our daughter. It seems like she hasn't changed a bit."

I chewed my lip.

How much of it was true?

I suspected a lot was, if not most of it. It sounded exactly how my mother would react. She would have taken three million dollars if it was offered. She was more ambitious than she was sentimental. But to make someone care about her, fall in love with her, then take the money and walk away? What kind of cold hearted bitch would do something like that? If that was the truth, then did I really know her at all? Did I even know myself?

I was starting to think I knew neither.

In spite of that, I said, "How am I supposed to believe what you're saying?"

"Ask your mother. She won't deny any of it. She lied to me since the day we met. I have to wonder if she's done the same to you. She never told you I existed. Never told you this life existed, if I guess correctly? She knew the moment I found out about you, I'd want to see you. Did she insist you move down to Dusk Bay? Did you never think the timing was suspicious, or sudden? It's because she knew what would happen. Everything she does, she does for her own well-being. If you got in her way, she'd climb straight over you, or shove you aside. People call me ruthless, but Helen was always much worse."

"She never locked me in a dark room," I pointed

out. She was my mother, she made plenty of mistakes, but she never did anything as horrible as that. At least, none I remembered.

"She sent you to me not knowing I knew who you were," he said. "Knowing you had no clue. Knowing if I caught you, I'd kill you. I'm sorry I locked you in there, but at the time I had no idea what your agenda was. Or if you knew about me. She might have spun some web of lies to make you hate me. She and the people she works with might have sent you to kill me. Once I realise your intentions were a lot more benign, I let you out."

"What about Frank Nixon?" I asked. The man Ice and I tortured to death would have happily killed me.

A heavy silence hung for half a minute.

"I don't know anyone by that name."

"He stalked me and admitted he wanted to strangle me." And worse, but I decided not to mention that. It didn't matter now anyway. "He said you sent him."

That same silence hung again. "I didn't send anyone after you."

CHAPTER SIXTEEN

KENNEDY

"Do you believe a word of it?" I was still snuggled up beside Ice, with Ares on the other side of me. Before the phone rang, I was sleepy. Now I was wide awake, a million thoughts bouncing around inside my head. "You guys have known about him a lot longer than I have."

I glanced over my shoulder at Ares. His body was pressed against mine, moulded into me like he wanted to crawl inside my skin. I couldn't see his face, but I knew from the sound of his breathing when the conversation irritated him. That was most of the time.

"We've been told about him." Ares sounded accusing, but I wasn't sure who it was aimed at. "I wouldn't say we *know* him."

"He's like the boogie man," Ice said. "Be good or Samuel Bell will get you. Don't say the wrong thing to the wrong people, or he'll get you. You never know who's listening. If word gets back to him, he'll get you. The walls have ears and eyes, and if they see you do anything wrong..."

"He'll get you," I finished for him. "Does that actually happen?"

I knew how easy it was to form a prejudice against something or someone. You only have to look at people's favourite car brand, or their desire to stick to only one type of phone. If you've spent a lifetime being told to hate something, that was usually what you did. Sometimes without questioning the reasoning behind it.

"He did lock you in that room," Mannix pointed out. He sat at the end of the bed, simmering with rage and frustration that threatened to bubble over.

I sat up a little and sighed. "I know."

My ability to hold grudges wasn't going to let go of that one easily. I still wanted to let Ice slice out Bell's kneecaps and use them as serving dishes. Or whatever people did with the kneecaps of torture victims.

"What if everything else he said was true?"

Mannix looked like he wanted to argue, but I went on.

"Consider the possibility for a moment. Charlie broke into the gym and was killed, but nothing was taken. No bombs were left behind. Maybe they *were* there to keep an eye on me."

That was still creepy as fuck, but better than thinking they were there for something nefarious, like killing all of us.

"Frank Nixon never named Bell as the person who sent him," I continued. "He said his boss wanted to send a message that they could get to Leo whenever they wanted to."

"Who else would it be but Bell?" Mannix's voice was tighter than a fly's ass. He, in particular, seemed to be struggling with the idea that Bell might not be as bad as his father always told him he was. His whole life was built on the foundation of the feud between the Bell and Brantley families. That belief was deeply ingrained into every fibre of him. If that was taken away, what was left?

"Does Leo have any other rivals?" I asked. "Maybe Nixon was sent by someone in Bell's employ. Someone who went behind his back?"

"If that's the case, they're not going to live very long," Ice said, sounding sleepy.

Mannix snapped his fingers. "Right. They won't. Bell will find them and make a public example of them. If they exist."

"You don't think they do?" I asked.

He rubbed a hand over the stubble on his chin. "Why go after Leo? Why risk going behind Bell's back to get at him? Leo is powerful, but there are much more powerful players in the game than him. Reuben, Caleb, their brother Joshua. Daisy Lasalle, Hilton Blake, Ric DiMarco. Hell, Mack D'Antonio is a bigger target than Leo."

I lay back down. "I don't understand any of this," I admitted.

"Bell was probably lying through his teeth," Mannix concluded. "It's what people like him do. They manipulate people to do what they want. Everything he said was just to make you doubt your mother, Leo, and us. That's it. He's trying to plant seeds of doubt and stir up trouble. And it's working."

"I guess so," I agreed. Mannix was right, it *was* working, whether it was some kind of manipulation or not.

"Maybe this isn't about Leo," I said finally. "Maybe it's Bell's attempt to get back at my mother. Like you said, he's trying to get me to doubt her."

That was working too. There was too much truth

in what he said. Wasn't that what made someone a good liar? Give the listener just enough truth that it gives credence to the lie. Let the listener do the rest.

"I need to talk to her. I need to know if what he said about my grandmother sending her after Bell, was true." I hardly knew the woman. She'd died when I was three or four. I had her name as my middle name. That was about the extent of it.

"You think she'll admit it if it was?" Ares asked. "No offence, but your mother seems to have her own agenda."

Usually I'd take offence to any words said after, 'no offence,' but in this case he wasn't wrong. I loved her, but my mother often prioritised herself above everything else. I didn't want to think she put herself before me, but the more I got to know her, the more I wondered if everything she did was about her and I was just along for the ride.

"Would she take three million dollars to stay away from someone?" Ice asked.

"I need to ask her that too," I said. "I don't know anything anymore. I don't know if my whole life was a lie."

"If yours was, then so were ours," Mannix growled softly. "But you know what, I don't want to talk about this anymore." He dropped to all fours and stalked up the bed towards me. "I don't want to talk at all."

"Really?" I eyed him. "What do you want to do?" As if I couldn't guess. He was insatiable. So was I. My body throbbed already.

"Everything," he said in a growl that set my body on fire. He lay over me and gripped my sleep shorts. With one jerk, he ripped them apart.

"Hey, those were new," I protested.

He grinned as he tossed both pieces away to either side. "I'll buy you more. Or not. You could sleep naked instead." He backed up his words by grabbing my singlet and tearing that too. "Clothes are overrated anyway."

"Finally, my dream is coming true," Ice said, a lazy smile on his face. "Mannix and Kennedy walking around all day naked." He glanced over to Ares.

"Dream on," Ares told him. "The world isn't ready for that much awesomeness."

"I think it is," I told him. I turned my attention away from him a moment later when Mannix slipped a hand between my thighs and up into my already wet, hungry pussy.

A shiver passed through me. Between his touch

and the way the other two were eyeing me like I was a tasty snack, round one might not last long.

I half expected the guys to touch me, or each other—a girl could hope—but instead they sat back to watch. Okay, I could roll with that. I liked them to look at me, it made me feel pretty. Gorgeous even.

Eyes half-closed, I watched them watching me while Mannix pushed me closer and closer to coming.

All three guys had matching expressions on their faces again, this time appreciating the show, and my body. There was something so overwhelmingly erotic about being the centre of attention like this. Something that drove me hard and fast.

Just before I came, Mannix pulled his hand back.

What the fuck?

I blinked at him and made a face.

He grinned. "Not yet."

"Tease," I growled.

That made him grin even harder. He waited until I came back down, almost all the way back to earth, before he started tracing minute circles around my clit with his fingertip.

The pressure rose again, more intense this time. I curled my hands around the bedcovers and dug my fingernails into the black cotton fabric.

Like before, when I was about to come, Mannix took his hand off me.

I growled at him, deep in the back of my throat.

Just like before, he was unapologetic. He fixed me with a firm look.

"You'll come when I say you can come. Not before. I meant it when I said your body belongs to me. Everything, including your orgasms. Especially your orgasms."

"Do you want me to beg?" I asked. Because I could beg. It was orgasms we were talking about here.

"That could be fun," Ares said. He looked particularly smug for some reason.

I stuck my tongue out at him.

He stuck his back out at me.

"So mature," Mannix said sarcastically. "Another day I'll make you beg, but today, you'll come when I say you'll come."

"Fuck, it's hot when you're bossy," Ice sighed. "Okay, it's hot when you're not bossy too, but this is totally working for me."

Mannix flashed a smile, then, because apparently he wasn't a complete asshole, he lowered his hand back to my pussy.

I watched his expression through narrowed eyes.

If he was going to edge me again, I was going to kick him in the nuts. On the other hand, who was I kidding? I was loving every minute of it.

I loved it even more when he said, "Okay, Princess, come for me."

And come I did, hard and fast. My whole body writhed and bucked, grinding against his hand. The thunder of blood through my ears, the heat of it coursing through my body was worth the wait.

I cried out nice and loud, so the whole house probably heard me. Whatever. I wasn't ashamed of any of this.

"Good girl." Mannix raised his hand to Ice's mouth and let him suck on his fingers.

"Fucking delicious," Ice groaned.

"I know you are." Mannix kissed him quickly, then nodded to me. "Get on all fours."

I did as he ordered. I looked back over my shoulder at him. He gripped my waist in firm, bruising fingers and positioned his cock outside my pussy. In true, merciless Mannix style, he slammed his cock into me as hard as he could.

I cried out in surprise, with a splash of pain, but no hint of complaint. I liked it when they were gentle and I liked it when they were rough. Everything they did to me, every touch was perfect and amazing.

Mannix slid his hands up to cup my breasts. My nipples were rock hard against his palms, eager for him to rub and pinch and squeeze. He did all of those things while pounding into me with firm, even strokes.

I wanted to suggest he couldn't come until I said he could, but I had no words, only groans, moans and pants.

"You feel fucking amazing, Princess," Mannix said breathlessly. "So perfect for my cock. So..."

Whatever else I was, I didn't get to find out, because he came, thrusting frantically and groaning deep and low as bliss claimed him.

He slumped over my back, panting and digging his fingers into my breasts. He stayed like that for a while until he caught his breath, then he slid out of me and flopped onto the mattress.

"My turn," Ice said. He pulled me over until I straddled his hips, then carefully lowered me down onto his thick, heated erection.

His hands on my hips, he helped me to rise and fall, up and down his length. My breasts bounced freely, nipples hard points begging to be touched.

I let him set the speed and rhythm, content to enjoy the way he felt inside me and how my clit brushed against him with each stroke.

He and the other guys were going to be the absolute end of me. And I couldn't get enough of it. Every time they touched me, I wanted more. Every time one of them had their cock inside me it was both enough and not nearly enough all at the same time. I would never, ever get tired of this.

"Beautiful, you feel delicious," Ice said breathlessly. "You make me and my cock both very happy." He looked over at Mannix with half an eye. "You too."

"I know," Mannix said with no hint of humility.

"You're such a dick," Ares told him, but his tone was affectionate rather than purely scathing.

Mannix grinned and went back to watching Ice and I slowly fuck.

Ice wiggled his hand in between us and rubbed my clit as he thrust up into me. "Come for me, Beautiful."

I groaned and angled my body so my clit grazed more firmly over his fingers. I waited for Mannix to tell me no, but he didn't. Evidently he was happy to let Ice be in the driver's seat for a change.

With no one to stop me, and Ice's eyes on me, I came, squeezing his cock so hard he couldn't keep from coming too. His eyes half closed in concentration and he thrust up and up, and up, until he fell still and groaned out his orgasm. His head lifted up off the pillow.

"Hell yeah," he breathed. "So... Fucking... Perfect. So... Ahhh."

He exhaled hard and his head dropped back down.

"I will never get tired of that." He opened his eyes and smiled at me.

"Me either," I agreed.

"My turn," Ares said.

I thought he might go for his paddle and spank me silly but instead slid me off Ice, and rolled me over onto my stomach. He grabbed my wrists and pinned them above my head with one hand. He lowered most of his weight onto me and pried my legs apart with his knees.

With as much mercy as Mannix gave me, he slammed his cock hard into my pussy. If it wasn't for the other guys stretching me for him, it would have hurt like hell.

It still hurt, but instead of crying out in pain, I cried out in pleasure.

He leaned down to whisper in my ear. "You like that?"

I made an incoherent sound, then said, "Harder."

"With pleasure." He pulled all the way out of me,

then slammed back in again, twice as hard as the first time. Hard enough to bring tears to my eyes.

"Harder," I said again.

He did, so hard I screamed. It was perfect.

Over and over, he drove himself deep into me. He held nothing back, not one centimetre, not one drop. He was soon breathing hard with the exertion, but never once did he thrust more softly. Never once did he give me anything more than everything, all the way to the hilt. All the way to his balls. They slapped against me with each stroke, a counterpoint to the wet sucking of his cock sliding in and out of my pussy.

"I'm going to fucking come inside you, Firecracker," he said with a grunt. "You're going to take every drop of me like you took every drop of Mannix and Ice. You'll be so full, you'll overflow."

Yes please. His words brought me back to the brink and over. I came harder and faster than I ever had in my entire life. If you asked me what my name was, right then I couldn't have told you. I couldn't have formed a sentence. Not even a word. All I knew was the throbbing of blood through my entire body and the cascade of pleasure. Nothing else existed in that moment.

After a million years in that beautiful space, I

started to come down. Just as Ares came, driving in with powerful, determined thrusts.

He didn't say a word, just let out a long, low groan, milking himself in the tight, wet heat of my pussy.

Finally, he slumped, his chest slick with sweat against my back. He still didn't speak, just held me while we caught our breaths in a tangle of arms and legs and satisfaction.

CHAPTER SEVENTEEN

"I'm not letting you go in there by yourself." I jutted out my chin and stared Kennedy down. She was a badass woman, but I wasn't backing down on this. "I'll tie you to my bed if I have to." She knew I would and we'd both enjoy it too.

She stopped with her hand on the door handle. "You can punish me later." Her eyes lingered on me as she turned away, a smile on the corners of her luscious mouth.

"I will punish you later, but I'm still not letting you go in there alone." I could, and I would, scoop her up, throw her over my shoulder and carry her off somewhere else. Then I'd fuck her so hard she wouldn't be able to walk, much less run away.

Now I thought about it, maybe I should just do

that anyway. My cock twitched, ready to leap to attention at a moment's notice.

She sighed. "Fine, but for fuck sake don't make the situation any worse than it already is."

I couldn't see how that was possible. "I'll try to behave. And if I don't, you can punish me." She could do that anyway. Any time.

She glanced back at me and rolled her eyes. She turned the handle and pushed the heavy timber door in on silent hinges.

I'd been in Leo's office a bunch of times, but it always struck me how big it was. The apartment I grew up in was approximately the same size.

Of course, we didn't have a huge, walnut desk, oversized leather chairs, or a view over the ocean.

Leo's house sat on the side of a cliff, leaving nothing but water and sky framed in a massive picture window. If this was my office, I'd get nothing done. I'd either be staring at the waves, or fucking Kennedy in front of the window, both in full view of the world and where no one could see us.

That thought made my balls heavy, so I pushed it away and turned my attention to Leo and Helen. They sat side by side in those oversized leather chairs, their heads together as they talked about fuck knows what. Probably something about how to screw someone over. Wasn't that what rich people spent their time doing?

Leo looked like an older, harder version of Mannix. Same dark hair, same intense eyes, but Leo's hair had a peppering of grey.

Helen's hair was a faded version of Kennedy's, but as far as I was concerned, that was where the resemblance ended. Her nose was sharper, lips not as full. Her breasts were smaller and her skin wasn't dotted with a million, adorable freckles. Her expression was harder too, bitter, like she was convinced the world had fucked her over somehow. She was still a beautiful woman, but paled in comparison to her daughter.

Right now, she and Leo were looking at us with curiosity laced with annoyance. More of the latter than there was of the former. Whatever, I wasn't going to apologise.

"I'm sorry to interrupt," Kennedy said. She didn't sound sorry.

When she first moved here, she would have meant it. She would have snuck back out the door and closed it behind her as silently as she could. No, she wouldn't have come in here in the first place. She would have waited until they came out and then asked to speak to them.

Us guys, we'd encouraged her to go after what she wanted and she was doing exactly that.

Good girl.

Leo put the piece of paper in his hand onto his desk and crossed his legs at the knees.

"It's not a problem, we always have time for you."

Those were the words that came out of his mouth, but his eyes said otherwise. To my surprise, he looked wary. Did he suspect we'd come in here to kill them or something? Should we have?

If Kennedy or Mannix wanted them dead, I had no trouble doing that for them. I was loyal to Leo to a point, but I was loyal to Mannix and Kennedy until the day I died. If they needed a thing done, I'd do it. No question.

"Where are the other guys?" Helen asked. She looked around us expectantly.

"They had some things they had to take care of," Kennedy said. "It's just us at the moment."

Mannix and Ice had to question someone at Ice's workshop. We both wanted to go with them, but Mannix insisted we stay here. Kennedy, to keep her safe, and me to keep an eye on her. I didn't mind being her bodyguard, even if it left me out of other kinds of fun. What was a little torture compared to spending time with a gorgeous woman? The woman

I fell hard for, to my surprise. I never expected to feel that for anyone. For a long time, I suspected I wasn't capable of love, just hate, anger and self loathing. The kid who grew up poorer than dirt.

Now, thanks to her, and my brothers, I stood on solid ground for the first time in my life. Brothers in arms, if not by blood. My family. My whole, fucking universe.

Helen looked relieved. She glanced at Leo. I could almost see the thoughts going through her mind. The two of them could deal with the two of us if they needed to.

Kennedy clasped her hands together and stood with one foot ahead of the other. The pose wasn't aggressive but it clearly said she expected to be listened to.

"I got a phone call last night," she said. "From Samuel Bell."

Leo and Helen's response was immediate. They both looked ready to jump out of their chairs. To do what, I don't know, but they were on edge. Jumpy. That made them both dangerous. We'd have to tread carefully.

"How did he get your number?" Helen paled. Her voice was high. Even if I wasn't trained to hear it, I would have. She was the little mouse now.

"I have a feeling you'd know better than I do," Kennedy said. "If people have enough money they can get whatever they want. How he got it doesn't matter right now. What matters was—"

"What bullshit did he try to feed you?" Helen asked. She was more composed now, ready to shovel bullshit. I trusted her as far as I could throw her. If she wasn't Kennedy's mother...

Kennedy licked her lips. "He said Grandma was working for the Brantley family. That was how you got into Brutham Academy."

Helen hesitated. "That's right. It's not somewhere you can simply apply to and get in. If you want Leo to put in the word for you..."

"I don't," Kennedy said quickly. "Bell also said Grandma wanted you to chase after him."

"She wasn't against it," Helen said carefully. "Sam was different then. He was sweet."

"He said you broke up with him when he said he was leaving the family and wouldn't have money," Kennedy said.

Helen snorted. "Of course he'd say that. He was convinced everyone was after him for his money. He could never accept that I was different. He was...paranoid."

"So you didn't take three million dollars to stay

away from him?" I asked. I couldn't help it, the question was burning a hole in my brain.

Helen glanced at Leo. If any of this is news to him, he gave no sign of it. I had a feeling he was in all of this up to his eyeballs too. Shady motherfucker.

"I tried to tell him about you," Helen said eventually. "His father stopped me and made me tell him instead. He said Sam was with someone else and offered three million dollars to look after you. I wasn't going to turn down money to look after my child."

"So you didn't take it in return for staying away from Bell?" Kennedy asked.

Helen shifted uncomfortably in her chair. "That was part of my deal with Sam's father. He'd give me the money to take care of you and I would stay away from Sam. Let him live his life in peace with Penelope. When she died a few years later, his father approached me to remind me of our deal. I said I'd stick to it, and I have. And because of that money, you had a good, privileged life. You've done a lot of things other kids couldn't. Things you wouldn't have been able to do if it wasn't for me making that deal."

She spoke as though she expected gratitude, and lots of it. She didn't get it. Not from Kennedy, and sure as hell not from me.

"Why did you send us to Bell's?" Kennedy said softly. "You knew how dangerous it was. What might happen if we got caught. We all could have died."

Leo rolled his eyes. It wasn't the first time I got the impression he'd be happy if the three of us guys were out of the way.

Helen actually laughed. "I didn't send you, you begged to go. You four insisted you could do it."

"What's really going on here?" Leo asked. "What are you accusing us of?"

Kennedy looked uncertain. "Bell said—"

"A bunch of lies, and you bought straight into them," Leo said. "And you've come in here accusing your mother and I of deceiving you in some way. So your mother didn't tell you who your father was, that doesn't make her suspicious of every little thing that ever went wrong in your life. I welcomed you into my home, into my family, and this is the repayment I get." He included me in the dark look that accompanied his words.

I didn't flinch, but Kennedy swallowed audibly. "I didn't mean to—"

"But you did anyway. What else did Bell say? That we suggested he lock you in that room?" Leo looked even more like Mannix now, face contorted with fury.

"No," Kennedy said quickly. "He said he sent people to look out for me and those people were who dealt with Charlie. He said he was trying to protect me."

Leo let out an ugly, barking laugh. "I knew you were naïve, but not that naïve."

I suspected he meant to crush her spirit a little, but it had the opposite effect.

"I'm not naïve," she insisted. "I'm just done being lied to. I feel like a fucking pawn on a chessboard, moved around back and forth wherever people think I should go."

"Watch your language," Helen snapped.

I was tempted to tell her to fuck off, but bit my tongue for Kennedy's sake. That would only make the situation worse, and Leo may try to kick me out of his office. If he did that, I might end up killing him after all, or at least, punching him in the face.

"What else did Bell say?" Leo asked coldly.

"He said he didn't send anyone after me," Kennedy told him.

"You saw the man with your own eyes," Leo pointed out. "He confessed what he did."

"He never said Bell sent him," Kennedy said.

"He implied it." Leo frowned. "Who else would have?"

"I don't know," Kennedy admitted. "His daughters?" She looked painfully uncertain. She reminded me of a doll whose hands were held by a pair of toddlers. One pulling in one direction, the other pulling in the other, neither having any intention of giving up.

"I wouldn't put it past that pair of snakes," Leo agreed. "Either way, they came from the same place. The Bell family. None of them can be trusted."

"None of them?" Kennedy echoed.

He realised the implication of what he said and his mouth opened and closed a couple of times.

"You know what I mean," he said finally.

"Do I?" she asked. "I have Bell blood running through my veins. Do I have any Brantley blood?" She glanced at her mother. "What about Cassani or DiMarco?"

"Not that I know of," Helen said. "But my mother did work for them for a long time, so anything is possible."

When Kennedy gave her a sideways look, she added, "It's unlikely. My parents had a good, strong relationship."

"Right. So I'm more Bell than anything else," Kennedy concluded.

"No, you're half Knight." Helen placed her hands

palm down on the arm of the chair and started to push herself to her feet. "Of course we trust you. Right, Leo?"

The fucker actually hesitated. Only a moment, but it was enough. Leo rose and put a hand on her arm. "Kennedy..."

She shook him off. "Don't. I got the message loud and clear."

She gave them both a scathing look, then turned and marched out of the room, her chin high, back straight.

I knew I was the only one in the room who heard the sound of her heart breaking.

I gave them both a dirty look and hurried out after her.

CHAPTER EIGHTEEN

KENNEDY

"Kennedy, wait!"

I ignored Ares and trotted up the stairs to my room. A few months ago, I would have been blinded by tears. Today, it was anger. I didn't believe for a moment Leo meant anything other than what he said. He was too deliberate, too controlled, to blurt out things he didn't mean.

I stormed into my bedroom and tried to violently shut the door behind me.

Ares grabbed it and stopped it before I got my satisfying slam. It wouldn't have made a sound anyway, I quickly realised. The doors were designed not to be slammed shut.

Fucking tantrum-proof design.

"Kennedy." He closed the door behind me. "What are you doing?"

I stomped into my ridiculously oversized walk-in wardrobe and grabbed the suitcase from the shelf above my skirts.

"If they don't want me here, then I'm leaving." I placed the suitcase on top of the chest of drawers and yanked the zipper open.

I shoved the lid up.

"Fuck." It fell back down on my fingers. I shoved it up again and started throwing in whatever I could put my hands on. Underwear, jeans, T-shirts, a pink sock. Fuck only knew where the matching sock was. Whatever, I didn't care right now.

"Kennedy," he said again. "Would you fucking stop?" He placed his hands on my shoulders, firm enough to stop me from continuing to pack. Not firm enough to turn me around until I was ready to look at him.

That took another couple of minutes.

Finally I turned around and looked up at him.

"Why? You heard them. They don't trust me. Leo can't look past who my biological father is, as if I can help who came inside my mother. Why isn't he blaming her for this? She was the one who kept it from him. From me. She lied to us both. To all of us.

Even if she wasn't a gold digger, she dug a hole. Who was the one who got buried in it? I did. Me."

He put his arms around me and let me hide my face in his chest. He was hard, solid and warm. He'd showered an hour ago, after swimming laps in the pool, so he smelled like musk and soap.

"Whatever problem they have, it's their problem," he said, his cheek resting lightly against my hair. "I think Leo is pissed at Helen, but he took it out on you because he doesn't know how to deal with someone he married five minutes ago. He's still thinking with his cock."

I grimaced. Leo's cock was the last thing I wanted to think about. Especially near my mother. Ewww, parent sex.

"Then I'll happily leave them to work it out," I said. "You don't have to come with me."

Okay, I held my breath. I *wanted* him to come with me. I wanted all of them to come with me. If they didn't, if they chose Leo's side...

"Of course I'm fucking coming with you," he said. "You don't get rid of Ares Turner that easily. I wasn't named after the God of war for nothing. It's because I always fight. I don't give in or back down. I'm not gonna start now."

I lifted my head and looked up at him. A watery

smile was better than watery eyes. I was *not* going to cry, no way.

"I don't know where we'll go," I admitted. "Or if the others will come with us."

"I'm always in favour of coming with any of you," Ice said. He stepped through the doorway, quickly followed by Mannix. They must have arrived just in time to hear me say that.

Mannix saw my suitcase and his eyes narrowed. "What in the fucking hell is going on?"

I explained in as few words as I could. His and Ice's faces turned redder and redder. Mannix's in particular. By the time I was done, he looked ready to burn the entire house to the ground.

"We're going with you," he said when I was finished. He nodded towards Ice and they both hurried out to pack their own suitcases.

"You should pack yours too," I told Ares.

"I'll help you with yours and then you can help me with mine." He pulled out that stray pink sock and threw it aside before opening my underwear drawer and emptying most of it into the suitcase. "There. All done."

I snorted a laugh and threw in as much of my clothes as I could fit. "I can't just walk around in my underwear."

"I'd prefer you naked," he admitted. "But you might need to leave...wherever we're staying, once in a while."

"If I walked around naked, you three would have to do the same." I closed the suitcase and drew the zipper shut before grabbing the handle and pulling it off the chest of drawers.

"You say that like you think any of us would have a problem with that." He grinned. "I'm not even wearing underwear right now." He grabbed his groin and his grin widened.

I just shook my head at him.

"Wasn't it you who said the world wasn't ready for all that awesomeness?"

If we were all naked all the time, how long would it take before they wore out my pussy? Yeah, they wouldn't need to be naked all the time to do that. They were working on it pretty well as it was. I was here for every moment of it.

He grabbed the handle from my hand and rolled my suitcase the rest of the way to the door. We left it there and hurried into his room to throw things into his case. Of course those things included his paddle, some rope, a pair of handcuffs, a different coloured pair of handcuffs, a ribbed vibrator and half a packet of TimTams.

I ate one of the chocolate biscuits while he folded several pairs of jeans and put them inside his black suitcase.

By the time we were done, so were Mannix and Ice.

Mannix's suitcase was black like Ares', but newer. Ice's was bright red and covered in images of various superheroes. Somehow, it was exactly the kind of suitcase I'd expect him to have. It was an interesting contrast to my sky blue suitcase, which was covered in stickers from my favourite bands and authors.

It shouted that I was a nerd, but at least I was a cool nerd.

Ares took the handle of my suitcase again and we made our way back down the stairs.

Staff moved around doing various jobs, but no one gave us more than a second glance. They were all used to us by now, coming and going and doing whatever. They probably assumed we were off on some mission for Leo. Judging by one or two of the glances, they hoped we wouldn't come back. The house had been in turmoil since I arrived. Presumably they were looking forward to a return to the peace and quiet of before.

Whatever it was they were thinking, I wasn't

going to dwell on it. For the sake of my sanity, I should try not to dwell on what Leo said either. But yeah, grudges.

We stopped at the door that led directly into the garage. I looked back over my shoulder.

It wasn't until we crossed the threshold that my mother appeared from the direction of Leo's office. She froze at the sight of us and frowned. That deepened when she noticed the suitcases arrayed around our feet.

"What in the world is going on?" She addressed the question to me, as though the guys didn't exist. She might wish they didn't, but that was too fucking bad. We belonged to each other and that wasn't going to change, no matter what my mother thought about it.

"I thought we'd give you and Leo some space," I said lightly. "You are still newlyweds. You should be enjoying the honeymoon period without a bunch of twenty-somethings hanging around, complicating things."

"Even if those twenty-somethings are awesome," Ice said.

She shot him half a glance. She couldn't even spare a full glance before her attention returned to me.

"You don't have to leave," she said. "This is your home. Yours and Mannix's." No one missed the double meaning in those words. It wasn't Ares's or Ice's home. Maybe she'd hoped all of the suitcases were theirs. If that was what she hoped, then she'd be shit out of luck.

"Are you and Leo planning to leave?" I said coolly.

It took a moment for her to realise what I was asking.

When my words sank in, she laughed as though I said something hilarious. "I didn't mean that you could stay because we were going. Let's sit down and have a talk and work things out."

"I'm leaving, Mum," I said simply. "It's time for me to live my life."

"Leo didn't mean anything by what he said." She started to look upset, annoyed. "Don't let one little slip of the tongue come between us all. I'm sure Mannix would prefer to stay here, with his father." She looked at him beseechingly. *Now* she admitted he existed.

"I go wherever Kennedy goes," Mannix said. "We all need a breather from each other."

"It's dangerous out there." Her gaze took us in, one after the other, clearly hoping someone would be on her side. And maybe slightly accusing, like it was the guys who talked me into leaving, not the other way around.

"We'll protect Kennedy," Ares said.

"We'll protect each other," Ice added.

"We should go," Mannix said. He jerked his head toward the car. Once the decision was made, he was impatient to get out of the place.

Mum was wrong, these guys weren't trouble, they were just impetuous. All of them jumped in with two feet, whether they could see where they'd land or not.

Mum put a hand out towards him, but stopped short of touching him. "Wait. Your father—"

"Made his choice," Mannix finished for her. "I hope you two are happy together. We'll be in touch when we get a chance." His expression silently added, 'if we can be bothered.'

"Maybe you should talk to him before we go," I said tentatively. The last thing I wanted to do was come between father and son. Whatever Leo thought about me, was between him and me, not him and Mannix.

Mannix shrugged. "He'll know how to find me if he needs to." He nodded and waved us toward his SUV.

Mum made a noise of frustration and dropped her hand to her side.

"I only did the things I did because I love you." She sounded so defeated, but she answered the question. If she had to choose between me and Leo, she'd choose Leo. Exactly as I expected her to.

I stopped before I climbed into the SUV and walked back to her. I gave her a quick hug and a kiss on the cheek.

"I love you too. I just need some space, that's all. Do me a favour and stay safe. If it's dangerous for me, it might be dangerous for you too."

If Bell was the monster they made him out to be, he might go after her. Although, I remembered the catch in his voice when he spoke of her on the phone. Whatever happened in the meantime, I suspected he really had loved her.

She hugged me back and stood with her shoulder leaning against the door frame. "Call me and let me know you're okay. And if you need anything, you know where to find me too."

I caught a hint of tears before she turned away and shut the door. For a moment, I thought twice about leaving, but then Ice patted the seat beside him and I hopped into the SUV and let the door close behind me with a clunk.

"Are you all right?" Ice asked softly.

I managed a smile. "I will be. Let's get the hell out of here."

"Yes ma'am." Mannix grinned over his shoulder, started the SUV and hit the button to roll the garage door up and out of the way.

"First stop, anywhere but here."

CHAPTER NINETEEN

KENNEDY

If I thought it was conflicted before, it was nothing to how I was now.

It was as though someone opened the lid on a thousand piece jigsaw puzzle, and threw the box, and all the pieces up in the air. And then took all the edge pieces to make it harder to put the puzzle back together.

I stared out the window of the apartment Mannix took us to, without seeing anything. We were right on the top floor, with a view over the city and the bay.

I barely noticed. I was too busy trying to sort through thoughts that rushed through my brain like a waterfall. They kept coming, but when I tried to catch them and work through them, they slipped away, pushed by the pressure of another. It left me gasping for breath. And maybe some alcohol.

"I don't know who to believe any more." My breath left mist on the window. It lingered for a few seconds before it dissipated. It perfectly summed up my life lately. Nothing seemed permanent. Nothing but my guys.

"You can believe us." Mannix stepped up behind me and wrapped his arms around me. "None of us would ever lie to you or try to use you."

I leaned back into him, comforted by the warmth of his rock hard body. "I know you wouldn't. You three are amazing. It's everyone else that sucks."

He chuckled, the sound coming from deep in his throat. "Yeah, I figured that out years ago. That's one of the reasons we were so hard on you when we first met you. The guys and I have been a team for a long time. We were all scared that letting you in would change that. Ruin it. What if you only wanted one of us and you split us up? We relied on each other for so long, we didn't want that to stop. You see it all the time. Guy meets girl. Guy stops giving a shit about his guy friends."

"But that wasn't how it went," I said softly.

"No," he agreed. "You fit in with us like..."

"A missing piece of the puzzle?" I asked, the

analogy fresh in my brain from my thoughts of only a few minutes ago.

"I was going to say a slice of pizza, but that works too." He chuckled again.

I laughed softly. "I love puzzles, but I prefer pizza."

"Me too," he agreed. "I'm sorry about what my dad said. He can be a stubborn asshole sometimes. I guess that skipped a generation."

I snorted a laugh. "Yeah, you're nothing like him whatsoever." Only a whole lot, but not in the ways that mattered. Mannix's heart was a hundred times bigger than Leo's.

"I'd never treat you like shit." He pressed his cheek against mine, stubble grazing over my skin. "I don't care where you came from, as long as we're not biological brother and sister."

I grimaced, remembering Ice's amusement at that thought.

"I don't think we have to worry on that score. The only chance of that happening would be if Samuel Bell was your father and you look too much like Leo for that to be possible."

"Thank fuck for that," he said.

"What do you believe?" I asked. "About all of this,

I mean. The things Bell said versus the things Mum and Leo said."

"Fucked if I know," he admitted. "I think things between your mother and Bell probably fall approximately in the middle of both stories. She went after him for his money and broke his heart. She might've cared about him too. It sounds like they had a bunch of shit working against them, and they let it split them up. I get taking money to take care of you. I mean, you take care of people you love, don't you?"

His tone was suddenly husky as emotion crept in.

"Yeah, you do," I whispered.

"I love you," he said in my ear.

My heart skipped a couple of beats then did a cartwheel or two. "I love you too. For the record, it wouldn't matter how much money Leo offered me. I couldn't stay away from any of you. I wouldn't."

"Hell no you wouldn't," he growled. "We wouldn't let you. We'd hunt you down to the end of the earth if we had to and bring you back."

Ice's words from that night so long ago popped back into my mind.

"I think, sooner or later I will find you. You'll come to me and then we'll deal with you. I'm going to enjoy knowing you'll spend every day wondering if

this will be the day when I catch my prey. If this will be the day when you end up in my trap. If this is the day I make you mine. I'm going to enjoy making you squeal, little mouse."

Where once the memory of those words filled me with fear, now they made me shiver with excitement. He'd made me squeal many times since then, always in a good way.

"I know you would," I said finally. "If I ever end up at the end of the earth, it's not because I ran away."

"Of course not," he agreed. "Why would my princess run away from this? " He pressed his semi-erect cock into my hip.

"I can't think of a single reason." I wriggled my hip against him until he groaned. "Who owns this place anyway?"

"Don't change the subject," he growled. He turned me around and cupped my cheeks with his hands. "But because I know you won't give up until you get an answer, I do. I bought the place about a year ago, for those times I needed to get away from my father. Or if I didn't want anyone to know I was in town."

I looked up at him. "You and the guys were here that night? After what happened with Eric during the masked ball? So if anyone found him and tried to trace it to you, Leo could claim you weren't in Dusk Bay."

He tilted his head slightly. "Exactly. We came back here to wash his blood off us. We talked about the little mouse who saw us, as Ice kept saying. He said he smelled a woman, and that you'd find us. If he was anyone else, I would have gone after you that night. I would have hunted you down. But Ice...he was adamant, and you know how he can be."

"He was right, I did find you," I said softly. Not long ago, the thought of them washing that man's blood away would have freaked me out. Now, it was kinda hot.

"Yep." Mannix smiled. "You turned up right under our noses." He glanced down for a moment, then back up again. "I'm sorry we scared you that night. If we had any idea you were there..."

"What would you have done?" I asked.

He smiled softly. "I would have taken you back into the ball and made you spend the rest of the night dancing with me. By the end of the night, you would have been mine."

"I'm yours anyway," I whispered.

I admit, that all sounded a lot more romantic than the way the night actually went. I would have enjoyed dancing with him, and letting him try to win me over. I might even have allowed him to succeed.

How different things might have been from the very start. Easier in some ways, but less interesting in others. Not to mention, if I never found those masks, or never saw them in the first place, I might still be in the dark about who the guys really were.

He brushed his knuckle over my cheek. "Yes, you are. Body, mind and heart, all belong to me. To us. And every bit of us belongs to you."

I smiled softly. I liked the sound of that.

"It's funny how things work out. If you asked me that night where I'd end up, I never would have guessed it would be here. With you three. The mysterious, masked men who cut a man's throat in the forest." Yeah, no one would have predicted any of that. What would I have done if they had?

Oh right, probably hop on the first train out of Dusk Bay and never look back. Thank fuck that wasn't how it turned out.

"When you put it that way, it sounds romantic." He smiled lopsidedly. "Like something out of a novel."

"A dark romance maybe," I said with a slight laugh.

"That's the best kind." He grinned. He brushed his lips over mine.

A thought occurred to me and I had to give it voice in spite of not wanting to know the answer. Not wanting to break the mood of the moment.

"Is Leo going to be pissed off with you for leaving?" I asked. "I don't want to cause any trouble between you and him."

I seemed to be good at that lately, getting between him and his father, between my mother and Leo. Would I be in the middle of Bell and my sisters too? I couldn't imagine a universe where Lila would ever want to acknowledge my existence, much less show me any sisterly affection. Honestly, the feeling was mutual, but still...

"If there's any trouble between me and him, it's because he caused it," Mannix said firmly. "He knows how I feel about you. He must have known any suggestion he made that he couldn't trust you wouldn't go down very well. Not with your mother and sure as fuck not with me." He sucked in an irritated breath. "I'll talk to him when I get a chance."

"Not if it's going to cause any trouble." I looked at him, silently pleading him not to do anything rash. "I'm sure he didn't mean anything by it. Can we let it go? Confronting him could make everything a hundred times worse."

I didn't know what someone like Leo would do to his son as punishment for pissing him off, but I could take a few guesses. Whatever it was, it wouldn't be pleasant.

"Don't worry about me," Mannix said dismissively. "I can stick up for myself." He sounded like he was very certain he was invincible. He wasn't and that was what terrified me. At the end of the day, we were all just regular people.

Okay, maybe not regular, but none of us was immortal and I didn't want to lose a single one of my guys.

"I know you can," I told him. "I don't want anything to happen to you. Is that so bad?"

"Nothing is going to happen to me," he assured me. He curled his fingers in my hair, pulled me to him and slammed his mouth onto mine in a fierce, possessive kiss.

Whether his plan was to shut me up or make me forget the conversation, it worked. The jumble of thoughts disappeared from my brain like steam. It might have manifested as condensation, because I was suddenly very, very wet.

He slipped his hands down my ass and lifted me

up until I wound my legs around his waist. He turned us around and pressed my back against the window.

"Princess," he murmured between kisses. "I'll never stop wanting you." One hand held me in place while the other slid up my shirt and across my flat belly.

"Same with you," I said breathlessly. I'd come a long way from the virgin the guys first met. Now I couldn't get enough of any of them. I couldn't imagine a time when a touch, a whisper, a kiss wouldn't make me wet. These three guys drove me wild and I loved it. I loved them.

He tugged down the front of my bra and pinched my nipple.

It was hard enough to hurt, but in a breathless voice, I said, "Yes. Just like that." It felt so incredibly good. Everything he did felt good, but I was in the mood for something extra, something rougher. I wanted to feel him everywhere.

He pinched again, harder this time.

I moaned. If he wasn't careful, I was going to come against his stomach, with layers of clothes between us. I wanted him buried deep inside me, his cock filling my pussy to the brim.

"Fuck." Ice spoke suddenly from behind Mannix.

"You can have your turn later," Mannix muttered. "Kennedy and I are—"

"I'll take my turn later, but that's not the problem right now," Ice said, his voice higher than usual. Frantic enough to make me look up and over at him.

His eyes were on the window.

"What?" Mannix snapped.

"Something out there is on fire," Ice said. "And it looks like exactly where the gym is."

CHAPTER TWENTY

KENNEDY

"Fucking hell."

By the time we arrived at the gym, the building was well and truly ablaze. Black smoke poured out the roof. Flames licked the sky. The heat was so intense, we couldn't have gotten within a block of the place, even if the police weren't keeping people out.

The air was already thick, hot and acrid. My eyes stung and watered from the smoke. The smell was going to cling to my nostrils for days. The sight—that would live with me forever.

"It's toast." I brushed tears off my cheeks.

Two fire trucks were parked outside, their crews hosing the building as best they could. At this point, all they could hope to was to stop the fire from spreading.

Of all the things that happened in the last few weeks, this made me feel the most defeated. I could make up with my mother, and get over all the things that were said and done. I could deal with what I'd said and done. But this... This was different. This was personal.

More than that, it was a loss for all the kids who enjoyed using the gym. They'd all be devastated.

I was devastated.

"Anyone want to take the bet that this wasn't an accident?" Ares asked. His tone held no hint of amusement, only anger that simmered like mine. The barely contained urge to swear loud and long, and maybe punch something.

No one answered him.

Not one of us thought for a minute this was anything but deliberate. Someone had come along and, just like that, set my business on fire.

The worst thing about it? The seemingly ever-growing list of people who might have done it.

No, the worst thing was the way the community relied on the gym. The way the kids did. Everything inside it was replaceable, but that would take time. Time these kids would be missing out. It was unfair to me, but it was even more unfair to them. None of them did anything wrong.

Ice slipped an arm around me and pulled me to him. "I'm sorry. This sucks, big time. We'll figure out who did this and make them pay for it. I don't mean with money."

That earned him a faint smile. "I didn't think you meant money. Can I get first dibs on the pliers?"

How slowly could I tear out a toenail? How much could I make it hurt?

I realised I was digging my fingernails into the palms of my hands and forced myself to relax slightly. Any more pressure and I'd make myself bleed. It wasn't my blood I wanted on my hands right now. I wanted whoever did this to suffer. I wanted them to cry and feel defeated like the cowards they were.

They fucked with me. I could fuck back.

"I've got something a lot more fun than those." He grinned. "I've got this—" He stopped talking when a couple of police officers walked past. He watched them, then mouthed, "I'll tell you later."

I nodded. This definitely wasn't the time or the place for talking about torture devices.

I admit though, he piqued my curiosity. What could be worse than I already saw? Was it worse than using a nail to put out someone's eye? Because that was literally the worst thing I could think of right now.

I had a pretty good imagination, but my knowledge of torture devices was lacking. A shortfall Ice was doing his best to rectify. He was very generous in sharing his favourite hobby, and work, with me. He was lucky he could do something he loved, and got paid for it. He was the poster child for job satisfaction. And it was much safer for him to be doing that than running around being a serial killer, or whatever else he'd have been doing if this life hadn't found him.

"I should let my mother know I wasn't inside," I said. So we didn't part on the best of terms, she'd still like to know I wasn't dead.

Right?

Honestly, I could use a hug from her right about now. After all that went down, she was still my mother. She loved me and I loved her.

In spite of that, I couldn't bring myself to call her. When I pulled my phone from my pocket, I tapped out a brief but concise text message and pressed send. I watched the screen until she read it, then ignored the phone when it rang. I'd talk to her later.

The phone stopped ringing, then started again a

moment later. She tried a couple more times, then apparently gave up.

Finally, she sent me a message that read, "Glad you're okay, sweetheart. Call me." That was it. Short and to the point. At least she wasn't worried about me.

I sighed and responded with a thumbs up emoji, in spite of feeling very thumbs down right now. And a whole lot of crying emojis.

On the outside, my eyes were more or less dry, but on the inside I was struggling to hold it together. If it wasn't for the guys, I probably would have lost it. It wasn't every day you literally saw something you loved go up in smoke.

Zero stars out of ten. Would not recommend. I wouldn't even wish it on my worst enemy. Whoever that was right now. Pick one. Bell, Leo, Lila... Hell, I didn't have a clue anymore.

"I guess it wasn't her then," Ice said. "People who do shit like this don't usually try three or four times to contact you."

It hadn't occurred to me my mother was involved in some way, but I was happy to follow his reasoning. If she did this, she wouldn't have responded so quickly. Those might be thin straws I clutched at, but I gripped on tight for dear life.

"I hate to say this," Ares started, "but Ice is right. Whoever did this is probably somewhere close by, watching our reaction." He looked around, then stuck his middle finger in the air. "Just in case."

Ice grinned and did the same.

Mannix rolled his eyes and shook his head at them.

"That only leaves a bunch of other people." I sighed. "Bell. My biological younger sisters. Fuck only knows who else at this point."

"You have more enemies than I do," Ice said admiringly. "Assuming they are enemies, that is. And assuming this is about you."

Mannix nodded his agreement. "The assholes could be trying to get back at us for something we did. The fire could have started in the gym we're rebuilding, not the gymnastics. I hate to brag, but I have an enemy or two." He actually looked proud of the fact, like he flexed mentally.

Mobster men.

Okay, men in general, but these ones in particular. They had absolutely no shame whatsoever. It was one of the things I loved the most about all of them. They lived each day as it came, right on the edge. It was exciting, apart from shit like this.

"More like three or four," Ares said with a grunt.

"Just off the top of my head, I can think of that many people who hate your guts. Give me a couple of secs and I'll think up a few more."

"Thanks," Mannix said sarcastically. "Love you too, bro."

Ares rolled his eyes. "I didn't say I'm one of them, I'm just saying you have enemies, that's all. So do I. We share most of the fuckers."

"It's nice of you to argue over who is more disliked than whom to make me feel better," I started, "but I have a feeling when all the ash has settled, they'll find the fire started in the existing space. Undoubtedly with some kind of accelerant. The security cameras will be toast too, but they probably fucked with the feed anyway."

When this was over, I was going to sit down and invent a better security system. One that couldn't be turned off whenever people felt like it. I was getting really tired of people messing with my stuff. Maybe the guys would help me rig one up that would shoot lasers at anyone who tried to fuck with it.

Yeah, there's that holding grudges thing again. Whatever, it was justified.

"You know what the ironic thing is?" Ice asked. "That people don't hate me. They think I'm the goofy sidekick to these two." He nodded towards Mannix and Ares. "But in a way, I'm more dangerous than both of them put together."

He paused again when the police walked past the other way.

"That is ironic," I said once the police were out of earshot. Almost as ironic as the fact people apparently hated me, when I'd spent most of my life studying hard and trying to do the right thing. Look where that got me. Three hot boyfriends and an inferno.

My life was one long moment of fucked up, crazy shit. Topped with a bunch of orgasms. Talk about conflicting.

My phone rang again.

I considered ignoring it, but when I glanced at the screen. I recognised the number.

I looked up at Mannix. He didn't need to ask, my expression told him everything he needed to know.

"Answer it." His tone was decisive, but he was clearly not happy about it.

With the crowds gathered around, and the police moving back and forth, to contain the gathering crowds, I decided it was better not to put the call on speaker phone.

I pressed the screen to accept and held it to my ear.

"Hello," I said warily.

"Kennedy," Bell said, his voice faint over the sound around me. "Are you all right?"

I slipped out from under Ice's arm and walked a few steps away so I could hear better. "I'm fine. Why?"

He was silent for a moment. I almost heard his eyes rolling.

"You think I wouldn't hear about an inferno at my daughter's business?" he asked. "I probably knew before the fire trucks were called."

"Did you start it?" I asked bluntly. That would explain why he knew before anyone else.

His response was immediate and firm. "No. I had nothing to do with it. If anyone who worked for me did, they might as well have locked themselves inside the gym. Their lives won't be worth shit."

"How am I supposed to believe you?" I wanted to, if only to cross someone off my list. If only because he seemed committed to convincing me he was in my corner. Maybe Leo was right and I was naïve, but I was getting tired of hating people, and being angry and scared.

"What would I have to gain by doing that?" he asked.

"Um, you'd upset me, get back at me for what I

tried to do to you, set my business back by months, if not years." If I decided to rebuild, that was. "With the added bonus of attacking the guys' gym they're building next door." There was probably more, but that was all I could think of right now.

"All good points," he said. "But I have no desire to do any of those things. If I came after those boys, I'd do it more directly than this. Arson is so...tacky. In addition, I own several businesses on the street. Putting them at risk wouldn't be very smart, would it?"

"That depends on what you want to achieve," I said. "Some people would consider it collateral damage. Those businesses are insured, aren't they?"

"Of course they are, but I assure you, it wasn't me. Nor was it anyone acting under my orders. Whoever did it, they waited until my people left before they acted. They were watching, presumably hoping to pin this on me. Or at least, to avoid having any witnesses."

The problem was, he made too much sense. He was good at doing that.

"If it wasn't you, then who was it?" I asked. "One of my delightful sisters?"

"It better not be," he growled. "They should be at school right now." His tone suggested if they weren't, they could also lock themselves in my gym for all their lives would be worth after this.

I almost felt sorry for them. Almost.

Even if he wasn't a monster, he was clearly not an easy man to live with. Maybe I was better off not growing up with him in my life. I'd never know the answer to that.

"I'm running out of people to blame," I said. "If you have any ideas, or suggestions, I'm listening. And don't suggest any of the guys did this. They wouldn't do it and, anyway, I was with them."

He actually chuckled. "If they did, I'd want front row tickets to whatever you did to them in retribution. I know some people refer to them as the Devils of Dusk Bay, but I doubt anyone has seen anything compared to a pissed off Bell woman."

"If this is a redhead thing—" I was really tired of people suggesting we had no soul or had horrible tempers or whatever. My hair colour didn't dictate my personality.

"This is an, 'I can see you're a strong willed, intelligent woman,' thing," he replied. "I suspect we're more alike than you think."

"I have to take your word for it, because I hardly know you," I told him.

"That wasn't my fault," he said quietly. "If I had my way—"

"Do you have any idea who did this?" I interrupted. "Enemy of the family I haven't met yet? Any more siblings I don't know about?"

"You have a stepbrother, although his mother and I aren't together anymore. Zachary wouldn't have done this, but he's also away at school. There's only one more person I can think of. An enemy of the family you *have* met."

I listened as he continued to speak. My blood turned colder and colder.

CHAPTER TWENTY-ONE

KENNEDY

"Are you sure about this?" I put a hand on Mannix's rock hard bicep.

"Yes," he replied curtly. He half closed his eyes and drew a breath in through his nose. He let it out through pursed lips, opened his eyes fully and looked at me. "Sorry, I shouldn't take it out on you."

"You weren't taking it out on me," I said lightly. "You're right to be...disconcerted. Bell said a lot of conflicting things. Potentially, all a bunch of crap."

"Yeah, well, we'll find out, won't we?" He kissed my cheek and gave the other guys a nod.

I laced my fingers through his. Slow, but determined, we walked out of the apartment and climbed into the SUV.

The drive was short, and we did it in silence, each lost in our thoughts. Except Ice, who seemed to be humming the theme song to the movie *The Omen*.

When I looked over my shoulder at him, he grinned.

Of course he was enjoying this. He was probably hoping to get his chance to shine.

That may just happen.

Mannix parked the SUV beside an empty building a couple of blocks from what was left of the gym. While the fire hadn't reached the businesses on either side, both the gymnastics and the construction of the gym were gutted.

We weren't allowed in yet to survey the damage, but according to the authorities, there was nothing left. Apparently their investigation was ongoing. Judging by the expression on the investigator's face, they'd rule the fire as an accident and walk away with however much they were paid to say that.

None of us were fooled.

I briefly wondered how much it would cost for the truth, but decided it wasn't worth it. Besides, they'd likely been threatened with their lives if they admitted it. That was literally a dead-end not worth pursuing. I hated to let it go, but this was Dusk Bay.

That was how things here went. Sometimes it worked in our favour, sometimes not.

Mannix unlocked the door and we stepped inside the cavernous space. He hit the light switch. Several lights in the ceiling illuminated the space.

"It's a blank canvas, as they say." He stepped aside to let us enter and looked around, his chin raised. "It should do for what we need."

It should have smelt dank and dusty, unloved and unused. Instead, the smell of lavender and some kind of cleaning agent hung in the air. The more I thought of it, the more I realised I shouldn't be surprised it was fresh. Mannix would have seen to it. We probably missed the cleaning crew by a matter of minutes.

As if he guessed what I was thinking, he said, "The place was full of dust and spiders. I wasn't bringing my woman into this space. Or my bros," he added at the last moment.

"I don't mind a few spiders," I said. In spite of what people said about Australia, it wasn't the wildlife that tried to kill me, it was other people.

"But I appreciate you being thoughtful enough to have it cleaned before we came here." I didn't want him to think I took anything he did for granted. Everything he did, he did for a reason. To take care of us. Being possessive and controlling was his love language.

He smiled smugly. "So, what do you think? Is it the perfect space, or is it the perfect space?"

I laughed at his question and took a minute or two to look around carefully. In spite of the phrasing, I knew he wanted an honest answer. If this wouldn't do, he'd find me another one. And another one. Until he found somewhere that would work for what I needed.

I had to be careful whenever I mentioned anything, in case he went out and got it for me. I mean, I didn't really *need* a private jet, so I kept thoughts like those to myself. Although, it was Mannix. If I had the thought, he'd figure it out. He was nothing if not astute when it came to reading people. All of the guys were. I guessed it came with the territory.

I tilted my chin and looked up. "The ceiling is high enough." I could already picture the silks hanging. Three, maybe four of them. None with dead bodies tangled in the polyester.

One side of the space could work for gymnastics equipment. The other for tumbling, trampolining and various acrobatic skills. A section at the front would be perfect for practising cheerleading. If I could find someone to teach it. Kids could come here to learn a variety of skills and have a great time doing it. I admit it, the thought was exciting.

"Are you sure there's nowhere for a climbing wall?" Ares asked. "Or an indoor pool?"

"We have both of those in the apartment building," I pointed out. None of the guys had stopped their daily exercise routine since moving there. If anything, they were working out more often. I joined them whenever I could. That would be easier since I finished my last uni class. I passed with a high distinction, so all I had to do now was officially graduate. My cybersecurity business would have to wait for a while. I wanted to rebuild the gym first.

"You can never have too many climbing walls or indoor pools," Ice said.

I rolled my eyes at him. "We're not having either of those here. Wherever you guys set up your gym, you can do what you like." I knew they wouldn't really interfere with this. Just like I knew they would let me interfere with their plans if I wanted to. But I wouldn't. I had my baby and was happy to let them have theirs.

Ice pouted playfully, but then grinned. "I love it when you get all bossy like that. It makes me want to ask you to chain me to the ceiling and use my tools on me."

"Be careful what you wish for," I told him.

That just made him grin even more.

We turned as the door rattled and opened.

Leo stepped inside, followed by my mother.

He looked around, appraising the space.

She hurried over to me to give me a hug. "I was worried about you. After what happened to the gym, I was hoping you'd come home. How absolutely terrible all of that was. Leo has been speaking to the fire inspector, trying to get some answers. He said they've been vague at best."

I bet they have, I thought. Funny how that goes.

I forced a smile. "It was a shock. They may never know what happened. I'm assuming there was an electrical fault no one knew about. It might even have started next door, with the construction. There were tons of power tools over there. It only takes one to ignite and boom. The whole thing is alight."

I didn't have to fake the sadness or frustration as I spoke, even though the words were blatantly ridiculous. Not one single person in the room believed it. Mum clearly wanted to, I saw it on her face.

I let her have it. For now. She'd know the truth soon enough.

"So this is going to be your new gym." Leo looked at me with guarded eyes.

I smiled as though nothing bad ever happened between us. "That was what Mannix was thinking, yes. He said he bought the building ages ago, and never quite knew what to do with it. It's bigger than the old space, so I think it'll be perfect. What do you think?" My tone was all dutiful stepdaughter, like I wanted nothing more than to make amends. Like we asked them here to build bridges.

He regarded me for a moment longer, then looked around again. "I'm no expert on gymnastics, but if you say it's a suitable space, I don't see why you shouldn't move forward with the rebuild."

"I was hoping you'd say that," I said sweetly. "I guess the fire wasn't such a bad thing after all."

"Maybe it was an omen," Ice suggested. "The universe telling you to spread your wings."

The smallest flash of irritation crossed Leo's face, but it was so brief I almost missed it. If I wasn't watching him, I wouldn't have noticed.

"Yes," I agreed. "It's like the universe took away something small with one hand and gave me something big with the other. With the added bonus that no one was hurt when the gym went up in flames."

"That's the important thing," Mum agreed. "The

place could have been filled with children. Just imagine what could have happened." She shuddered. "What would have happened if you were in there? I could have lost you." She brushed tears off her cheeks.

The hug I gave her was genuine. I needed it as much as she did. It felt good to touch her, smell the rose scent she always wore. When was the last time we really connected like this? Too long.

"You didn't lose me. No one was hurt. We're all fine. Besides, you can't get rid of me that easily."

She leaned her head against my shoulder and I held her while she cried for a minute or two. When her soft, silent sobs finally subsided, she lifted her face and sniffled.

"I'm so sorry I dragged you into everything. Right from the start, I should have stepped away from all of this. We had that money, we could have started a completely new life somewhere else. Anywhere else."

If someone offered her time machine in that exact moment, so she could go back and change the past, I didn't think she'd hesitate. That was one difference between us. I held a grudge, but I didn't hold on to regrets. You couldn't change what happened in the past, no matter how hard you tried.

All you could do was move forward and work with the situation whether it was created by you or someone else. And maybe pull out a few toenails here and there.

I suspected Mannix would disagree. Not the could change the past, but that you shouldn't let anyone create situations for you. Whatever happened, wherever he went, he liked to be in the driver's seat. I couldn't imagine a time he'd step back and let anyone else take control. He was alpha through and through. A force of nature. He'd bring the destruction, then make a path through it for the rest of us.

"I have a funny feeling I would have been sucked into it sooner or later." I offered her a small smile. "The universe would have brought me to these guys," I jerked my head toward Mannix, Ice and Ares, "one way or another."

"Damn right it would," Ares said. "Either way we would have hunted you down."

"Even if we had to kidnap you and keep you tied up until we convinced you," Ice said.

Mum gave him a funny look, but smiled. "I'm sure you would do exactly that too. You all seem smitten with my daughter."

"She's the best thing we have," Mannix said. "Her

and each other." He gave his father a look. His face was almost expressionless, but there was something burning in the back of his eyes. For a moment there, I almost would have sworn I saw flames dancing in there. Any minute now, they'd shoot out and engulf us all.

"Young love," Leo said sarcastically. "You think the world would end if you broke up. It won't."

"We're not going to break up," Mannix said. "There's something else we want to show you." He gestured towards the back of the space. "Something I know you'll approve of."

Leo looked sceptical, but followed him into the back corner, where the ceiling lights barely reached.

I hooked my arm around Mum's and walked behind the others.

"Like Kennedy said, I bought this building a while ago. I wasn't sure what to do with the space up here, but there's an extensive space below."

I've never seen a smile as dark as the one that graced Mannix's lips at that moment.

He pulled a key out of his pocket and unlocked a door in that back corner.

I half expected it to creak as he opened it, but it moved on silent hinges, opening onto darkness.

Mannix leaned in and clicked the lights on over a set of stairs that led down.

I wasn't sure who looked more nervous, Leo or my mother.

I squeezed her arm. She'd know what this was about soon enough.

Mannix started down the stairs and the rest of us followed.

CHAPTER TWENTY-TWO

KENNEDY

This was my first time down here, but the guys told me what to expect. It was still impressive. At least twice the size of Ice's present workroom, but somehow less dank, in spite of also being underground.

Several brand-new sets of chains were bolted to the ceiling, each approximately two metres apart. Brackets for more were set into the wall. Three chairs were screwed into the floor, also two metres apart. Here and there were a bunch of other devices, the uses of which I could only guess at. They looked nasty.

In the centre of the room was what looked like nothing more horrifying than a kitchen island. It was topped with stainless steel and had drawers all around it. A double sink was set into the surface.

"I wanted a stove, but Mannix said no." Ice gave him a sideways look.

Mannix rolled his eyes. "You have that." He nodded towards the wall. Inset into the concrete was what looked like the kind of oven they used in cremations.

"I bet you the first thing that goes in there is pizza," Ares said.

"Now you mention it, that's exactly what I'm using that for." Ice grinned. "Disposing of evidence and cooking pizza. Ares, you're a fucking genius." He slapped Ares on the back.

Ares waved him away. "No shit. Of course I am."

"This is all very interesting," Mum said uncomfortably. "I've never seen...this side of things before."

"You don't know what you're missing, Mum," Ice said cheerfully. "I can call you Mum, right? I mean, you're my girlfriend's mum so—" He shrugged.

She gave him an awkward smile, like she wasn't quite sure where he fit in a space like this. "I suppose that's all right, Isaac."

"If I'm going to call you Mum, then you should call me Ice." He gave her a big hug. After a moment, she hugged him back.

It was the sweetest thing I saw all day.

"This is impressive," Leo said. "But I don't recall giving the authority to make another torture room."

"You didn't," Mannix said coldly. "I did. I wanted you to know I had everything under control when I took over from you."

"That won't be for a long time," Leo said. He eyed the chains nervously.

"Maybe not," Mannix agreed. "But maybe it will be soon." He walked towards his father, his steps slow but deliberate.

Leo backed up. "What do you think you're doing?"

"Good question," Mannix said. "But I have better ones. When did you find out Kennedy was Samuel Bell's daughter?"

Leo's jaw twitched. "When Kennedy told us." He didn't meet Mannix's eyes or mine.

Ice made a noise like a game show buzzer. "Incorrect. Try again."

Leo shot him a venomous look, but quickly returned his gaze to Mannix. "I'm not sure what you're trying to imply here."

"I'm not implying anything," Mannix said. "I'm saying you knew before Kennedy told any of us. I'm saying you're the one who sent Frank Nixon after her. I'm saying a lot more than that, but I'm giving you a chance to defend yourself."

Mum frowned at Leo. "Leo? Did you know?"

He scoffed. "Of course not."

Mannix nodded to Ice and Ares.

Both guys closed in on either side of Leo. Before he could react, they shoved him a handful of steps back to the chains. He writhed, grunted and tried to pull away, but they grabbed his arms, hauled them up and snapped manacles around his wrists.

"What the fuck do you think you're doing?" he growled.

"This." Ice walked over and pressed a button on the wall. The chains started to rise, pulling Leo's hands up higher above his head.

"If you won't tell us the truth voluntarily, then we're going to have to use more drastic measures," Mannix said. His voice was colder than a blizzard. He *was* the blizzard. Anyone caught in his path was fucked. The time for deceit was over.

I would have hated to be at the receiving end of his icy fury.

Mum looked panicked. "Kennedy, I didn't—"

"I know you didn't," I said quickly. "You would never do that to me." I hadn't thought Leo would either, but here we were.

I could see him scrambling, trying to think of what to say and how to get himself out of this. At the same time, he was getting angrier.

"If you think for a minute you can get away with doing this to me, think again. All four of you will pay for this." He shot daggers at Mannix with his eyes. They looked like toothpicks compared to Mannix's expression.

Mannix was pissed off with his father and wasn't going to be intimidated by him. Not anymore.

"Kennedy, did you have dibs on the pliers?" Ice opened a drawer and pulled out a set. He offered them to me but I shook my head.

"Under the circumstances, I think I'll leave it to the experts."

He nodded graciously and stepped away. He approached Leo, opening and closing the pliers as he went.

"Let's start again," Mannix said with an unusual display of patience. "When did you know Samuel Bell was Kennedy's father?"

Leo eyed the pliers, fear creeping onto his face. "I —" His throat bobbed as he swallowed. "I've always known. I was at Brutham Academy with Helen. I knew when she was involved with Sam. I lost track of her for a while, but when I found her again, she had a kid. It didn't take a genius to work out whose it was."

"But you chose not to tell anyone," Mannix said.

Leo's tongue swept over his lips. "I decided to sit on the information until it became useful."

Mannix nodded. "Why did you send Frank Nixon after Kennedy?"

"Leo would never do that," Mum argued. "Kennedy is like a daughter to him. Right, Leo?" She looked as though she wasn't sure what to believe, or who, but she desperately wanted answers.

"He wasn't supposed to hurt her," Leo said, his voice low as though he didn't want to say the words out loud. "He was supposed to scare her."

"He did that," I said. "He said he was sent to kill me. To show you his boss could get to you anytime he wanted to."

"He was told exactly that," Leo confirmed. "That was all he knew to say. People like him, they don't need to know all of the facts. They're there to do what they're told."

"Just a worthless drone to send to their deaths," Ares said coolly, meaningfully.

Leo looked him straight in the eyes and said, "Exactly."

Ares snarled and might have lunged at Leo if

Mannix hadn't raised his hand and indicated for him to stay back.

"That's all any of us are to you," Ares said bitterly. "Pawns in your twisted fucking game."

"You're exactly what you want to be," Leo said. "Exactly what you signed up for. Money, power, obedience. Don't pretend it bothers you now."

"I'm not pretending, asshole," Ares snapped. He stepped away, grumbling under his breath.

"You sent someone after my daughter?" Mum looked disbelieving.

"I needed her and the boys to believe Samuel Bell did it," Leo told her. "I needed them so angry they'd go after him. So angry they'd want revenge. Anything less and they wouldn't have been fully committed."

"You set it up so someone would almost kill my child, for the purpose of sending her and her boyfriends to a place that also might have gotten them killed?" Mum's face turned all tiger mother angry.

I thought she might grab the pliers from Ice and use them on her husband herself. Look, I can't say I'd try to stop her.

"I knew Bell must have known by then that Kennedy was his," Leo said, unflinching. "He would have been watching out for her, so he could tell her himself or whatever fucked up game he decided to play. I wanted the four of them angry enough that they wouldn't listen to him. Or believe him. If they did, it would weaken them and their mission. Put them at risk."

"Like you give a fuck if we're at risk," Ares snarled. "If we died, you wouldn't shed a tear."

"If *you* died I wouldn't," Leo told him. "Except the money I put into your training would be wasted."

"I'm starting to think you're not very nice," Ice said. "You'd be sad if I died, wouldn't you?"

Leo just looked back at him.

It was probably better he didn't answer, since Ice stood with an implement of torture in his hands.

"We're not supposed to be nice," Mannix said. "It's who we are. But we don't screw each other over."

"No, but we do screw each other," Ice said.

Mannix glanced over and nodded to indicate his agreement with that statement.

He walked back and forth in front of Leo a few times before he stopped and said, "What about the fire?"

Mum gasped. "He wouldn't..."

Leo must have known by then how fucked he was, because he didn't hesitate anymore.

"That was directed at Kennedy. From the moment that *bitch* came into our lives, she's turned everything upside down. For a while, I thought we could ride out the storm, but when she made Mannix move out, I was fucking done."

"I didn't make anyone move out," I said coldly. "You made it clear what you thought of me and I left. The guys made up their minds. If there's any kind of gap or rift between you and Mannix, it was there long before I turned up."

I stepped towards him. "It's there because you don't see him as a son. You see him as a chess piece you can move around however you want. And if he gets knocked out of the game—" I shrugged. "No big deal. Right? You just hand everything over to your other son or whoever the fuck else."

For once, my mother didn't tell me to watch my language. She was too busy gaping at Leo like she was staring at a stranger. She might as well have been. He was far from a nice guy. He was every bit the mobster. Dangerous, ruthless, remorseless.

"Did you ever care about me?" she asked softly.

He turned to her. "Of course I did. I do. I love you. I only did what I did for the good of the family. And because I was—"

Mannix interrupted. "If you say because you

were following orders, I will have Ice rip off your eyelids. Yeah, there are orders you need to follow, but you have enough autonomy that you don't need to fuck with me or the people I love in order to follow them. You could have told Kennedy who her father was and we would have thought of something else. There was no need for all the bullshit you did to her. None of it."

He stepped away, then moved back again. Every part of him was tightly controlled, from his movements to his expression. He knew exactly what he was doing.

"You know what? I understand why you did what you did. It's how we operate, isn't it? Do whatever you have to do to get what you want and don't let anyone stand in the way." When Leo started to interrupt him he snapped, "Shut up. It's my turn to speak."

He was silent for a minute or two before he continued, "You had a job to do and this was the best way to do it. To convince us. To avoid putting us in a position of vulnerability. To give us the best chance of succeeding."

"Exactly." Leo started to look hopeful. He might just escape this without being tortured. "I was doing what had to be done."

Mannix nodded. "I can respect that. The fire... you just got angry, right? No one was hurt and it turned out well because upstairs is a much better space. So in a way, you did us a favour." His voice was so tight I was surprised it didn't snap in two.

Leo nodded vigourously.

"But you did something unforgivable," Mannix added. "Something unnecessary. Something I don't tolerate, and neither does Ares or Ice. And you did it in front of Ares."

Leo looked confused.

Mannix slipped a hand into his pocket and pulled out a gun.

"You touched Kennedy."

He raised the gun and shot Leo twice in the left side of his chest.

CHAPTER TWENTY-THREE

"You killed Leo Cassani." Caleb's words were delivered as a statement, not a question, but he clearly wanted an answer.

"I did." Mannix met his gaze without wavering or flinching.

I didn't know how he did it. Personally, I wanted to pee my pants. Everything since Mannix shot Leo went by in a blur. The guys disposed of his remains. Mannix immediately contacted Ric DiMarco and told him what he'd done. We ate and slept and existed for two days until we got the call to come here.

The house Daze shared with Ric and Gunnar, and Hilton when he was in town, was big and imposing. Tastefully decorated, of course, and opulent, but the presence of Caleb and his older brother Reuben made being here nothing less than intimidating as fuck.

All of them reclined in armchairs, looking like judge, jury and executioners, even Daze, who greeted me like an old friend.

So far, Reuben hadn't said a word. He merely sat and watched the proceedings, and expression of mild irritation on his face. He was handsome, for someone twice my age, and he had that air about him. The one that suggested if he told a woman to get on her knees, she'd do it without hesitation. And he knew it.

"Why?" Caleb demanded.

In the same monotone voice, Mannix said, "Because he wasn't acting in the best interests of our family or the organisation."

My gaze wandered across the room and settled on Gunnar, Mannix's older brother.

He looked troubled, and grieving. Conflicted at the same time. Leo was his father, but he clearly wanted to believe Mannix wouldn't have killed him if he had a choice. That was better than him immediately assuming Mannix was in the wrong and baying for his blood. Daze had a hand on his knee, suggesting they'd had this conversation at least once in the last couple of days. Daisy Lasalle seemed like the kind of person who would encourage him to hear his brother out, for both their sakes.

"Explain," Caleb said.

Mannix did, in as few words possible. He described how Leo sent Frank Nixon after me and set fire to the gym. He didn't mention killing Leo because he touched me, or any bitterness for sending us after Bell. We'd discussed all of this and agreed none of that mattered. Caleb would only want to hear how Leo wasn't acting in his and Reuben's interests.

Caleb looked more and more annoyed as Mannix spoke.

"Does Leo's widow want retribution?" Caleb asked.

It was me who answered that question. "No. My mother agrees what Leo did was unforgivable and is grateful his execution was quick." She had a lot more to say than that, and a bunch of tears, but that was the gist of it.

In the end, she chose me over Leo.

"Gunnar Cassani, you've previously said you don't want to take over your father's interests." Caleb turned to Mannix's brother.

Gunnar shrugged one shoulder, but shook his head. "I have enough responsibility as it is. I'm happy to let Mannix have it. Dad's will was more than generous to me."

Caleb glanced over to Reuben, who nodded.

"All right then. Mannix Cassani, you can take your father's place in the organisation. I expect you understand your responsibilities and that we expect you to always behave and act in the best interests of the organisation."

Caleb fixed him with an intense expression that held an underlying threat no one missed. If Mannix put a toe out of line, especially in the next couple of years, they wouldn't hesitate to take him out.

"I always have and I always will," Mannix stated.

Caleb nodded. "Then there's one more order of business. The biological paternity of Kennedy Caroline Knight."

I winced. Did he have to bring my middle name into it?

We'd already rehearsed this. I lifted my chin. "My loyalty is with Mannix and this organisation. However, I'd like permission to maintain contact with Samuel Bell, in the capacity of an intermediary between the two families. We believe I might be able to intercede before any further blood is shed on either side."

Neither Caleb nor Reuben tried to hide their scepticism, but Reuben finally spoke.

"Under the condition all interactions are held with full transparency. If you're seen to act outside our interests, steps will be taken to remove you from the situation."

That was the most diplomatic way I'd ever heard anyone say they were going to kill someone else. I wondered if either Brantley brother ever let their hair down, or did they leave that to their youngest brothers?

"I understand," I said finally. "I don't foresee seeing, or speaking to, him without one of my guys present. If not all of them."

Reuben nodded. "See you don't." He stood and left the room without another word.

Caleb nodded to Ric and Hilton and did the same.

It wasn't until then that the air in the room relaxed, almost visibly.

Daze hopped up from her chair and came over to give me a hug. "I'm so glad that turned out okay. I really hate having to ask the staff to clean blood off the hardwood."

I wasn't sure if she was joking or not, but I

hugged her back. "Did you think they'd execute us for what happened to Leo?"

"It's impossible to tell," she admitted. "Some days they'll order someone killed, just because they're in a bad mood. Fortunately, you caught them both on a good day."

I stared at her for a moment. "If that was them in a good mood, I'd hate to see them in a bad mood."

She laughed. "Right? They aren't the friendliest men at the best of times."

Hilton gave her a look, complete with arched eyebrow, as though she said something treasonous, which she probably had.

She responded by being unruffled and blew him a kiss. "He can't say it's not true." They clearly adored each other.

I suspected she got away with a lot. I wanted to be her when I grew up. I had three adoring guys, but none of us were in the position to say whatever we thought, or do exactly whatever we wanted. Not yet.

Although, now we were only a step below her and her guys. I knew Mannix intended to do everything he could to stay there. We had power, influence and all of Leo's assets behind us. We were as close to untouchable as people got. It would be very easy to get intoxicated on all of it.

Daze took my arm and led me aside. "Is your mother really okay? I have a daughter myself and if any of my guys sent someone after her, he'd be lucky to get the quick death Leo got. In fact, I'd happily hand him over to Ice and tell him to make sure he lives for as long as possible. And as horribly as Ice can make his last days. No one messes with my kid."

I believed every word she said. It didn't matter how much she adored Hilton, Ric and Gunnar, they'd pay dearly if they did what Leo had.

"I'm not sure if I'd say she's okay," I said slowly. "She genuinely cared about Leo. She's still in shock over everything." For someone who had been embedded in this life since she was my age, seeing Leo shot in front of her was still incredibly difficult and confronting.

As for me, it replaced masks and dark rooms in my dreams. Dreams that weren't as bad as the nightmares. My subconscious must have known it was the only way that day was going to end. Known and accepted it.

Part of me wanted to feel bad, but as the guys took Leo out of the chains and hefted him into the hot oven in the wall, all I felt was relief. He got what was coming to him and Bell pointing the finger at him turned out to be right.

Until Leo admitted what he did, I wasn't sure chaining him in Ice's new workroom was the right thing to do. If Bell was wrong and Leo was innocent, we might well be the dead ones now. Leo wouldn't have forgiven us for our assumption or restraining him the way we had.

We'd rolled the dice and thank fuck the gamble paid off. We could have paid dearly. Leo's attitude to me tipped me off that maybe he did the things Bell suggested he did. None of the guys took much convincing. That was how they lived. Whatever they did, they were all in.

"We're taking good care of her," I added. "All of the guys adore her. She lost her husband, but she gained three sons." Ice, in particular, adored her. He followed her around the apartment, making sure she had fresh coffee and warm slippers. He even went out and bought her several new pairs of bed socks.

I told him it wouldn't be winter for another few months, but he shrugged it off and grinned in true Ice fashion.

"It's never too early to get ready for winter. And look, this pair has ducks all over them. I couldn't resist. Don't worry, I bought things for you too. Lacy things. I would have brought some for Mum too, but according to Ares, that would be weird." He shrugged.

He would never be anyone but his own, unique self, and we all loved him for it.

"That's awesome." Daze smiled. "Nova loves having three fathers. If one says no, she goes running to another one of them. Although, they don't tell her no very often. She has them all wrapped firmly around her little finger." She held up her pinky.

I laughed. I bet if the guys and I ever had children, the same thing would happen. They'd have an abundance of love and attention. What more could anyone want for a kid?

Children were a long way off for me, if we ever had them at all. Right now, I had enough to deal with without bringing a little human into the world.

"I should go before Reuben and Caleb upset the staff." Daze made a face and hurried away after I nodded.

I wondered if upsetting the staff meant leaving them in tears, or on their knees. Maybe both.

"We did it." Mannix stepped up behind me and slipped his arms around me. Ice and Ares did the same, until we were all enveloped in a group hug.

"Yes, we did," I agreed. "We get to live another day or two."

Mannix chuckled. "I'm the head of my family, just like it was always supposed to be. And I have my girlfriend, my boyfriend and my bro."

"Boyfriend," Ice echoed. "I like the sound of that."

"I like the sound of bro," Ares said softly.

He'd been quieter for the last couple of days. He'd seen Leo as a kind of father figure. Realising Leo didn't see him as any kind of son clearly stung. He didn't break down and cry like my mother had, but I caught him several times looking out the window, his lips pressed together so tight they were almost white. I could almost forgive the things Leo did to me, but not this. Ares was a self-proclaimed badass motherfucker. Leo turning on him was not all right. It wasn't the way you treated someone who looked up to you.

"And I have three boyfriends," I said.

"I really, really like the sound of that," Ares said.

I looked him in the eye and said, "You'll always have us."

He smiled. "Fuck yeah I will. I'm not letting any of you go."

"I love all of you," I said.

"We love you too." Ice pressed his forehead to mine.

"Yes we do," Mannix agreed. "And the four of us have some celebrating to do."

CHAPTER TWENTY-FOUR

KENNEDY

"We thought there was something you should deal with first." Ares held a black cotton drawstring bag in his hand.

I sat on the edge of the couch and eyed him doubtfully.

"Who is 'we'?"

"All of us." He flicked a finger in the direction of Mannix and Ice. "But it was my idea."

"If this goes badly, it was definitely your idea," Mannix agreed.

Ares flipped him off.

"We were all in on it." Ice gave both of them a look, then turned his gaze to me. "If it goes badly, it's the fault of all of us."

"Please tell me there's not a disembodied head in there." I grimaced. The bag was big enough.

The guys shared a glance.

"Not a head, no," Ares said slowly.

"Hunter and Parker Brantley's cocks?" I guessed. Honestly, I didn't want those either.

"Maybe you should just show her," Ice suggested.

"Yes, maybe you should just show me," I agreed.

Ares teased the bag open. He put his hand inside and pulled something out.

My heart stopped for a second or two.

"I told you this was a bad idea," Mannix said.

"No," I said quickly. "It's okay." I reached for the mask. It wasn't the one Mannix wore the night they killed Eric Parcell, but I recognised it anyway.

I looked up at Ares. "This was yours?" It was dark purple, with swirls on the forehead and the cheeks. Understated, like its wearer.

"Yeah." Ares shrugged. "I figured if you saw them up close and personal, they wouldn't be so freaky."

"Facing my fears and stuff like that." I turned the mask around in my hands. In this context, it was nothing but plastic, with elastic to hold it in place. Nothing scary at all, except some residual unease about that night. That was what this was about. Putting that unease to rest, once and for all.

"Exactly," Ares said. "You're not scared of much, but these masks made you run away once. I didn't want you to find them again and take off."

I glanced up at him and smiled. "I wouldn't, but I appreciate you doing this for me. Would you put it on?" I handed it back to him.

"Whatever my Firecracker wants." He placed the bag on the coffee table and pulled the mask down over his face. It sat just above his mouth, leaving his grin exposed. "See, totally harmless."

"Yes, you are," Mannix teased.

Ares rolled his eyes at him. He snagged the bag back up and dove back in again. He pulled out another mask.

This one was gold and black, and looked like some kind of cat.

"Ice's." Ares handed it to him.

Ice pulled it on and gave me a rakish smile. "Well hello there, little mouse."

It wasn't until then I realised the irony of his mask. Cat and mouse. Where once I would have been freaked out, now I laughed softly.

"Should I pour you a saucer of milk?"

He grinned. "I'd prefer cream." He slid over to Mannix and ran a hand over the front of his jeans.

"Soon, pussy," Mannix told him. He held out his

hand. Ares pulled out his mask and handed it to him. He turned to me and pulled it over his face.

This one was definitely the creepiest one of all. Not just because I saw it that night, or on my mother's wedding day, but because it covered his mouth with a very Mannix-like sneer. It reminded me of when we first met. He'd looked at me like he hated me on sight. The feeling was more or less mutual at the time.

Now, I didn't hate him and I wasn't afraid of the mask. Or any of them.

"Better, Princess?" Mannix asked.

"Much better," I agreed. When he reached to take it off, I put out a hand to stop him.

"Can you leave it on?" I looked at the other two. "You too. Just for a little while."

Mannix put a hand on the back of my head and drew me closer to whisper in my ear. "Are you saying you want us to fuck you while we're wearing these?"

I drew my lower lip in between my teeth and thought while I let it slide loose. "Would that be weird? Because I think it would be kinda hot." They killed a man in these masks. They made the guys look sinister, dangerous. Sexy.

"Whatever my Princess wants, my Princess gets,"

Mannix said. He reached down to tug my t-shirt up and over my head. My bra quickly followed.

I grabbed the hem of his shirt and yanked. He slid his arms out and placed his hands over his face to hold the mask in place while I pulled it off the rest of the way.

"You know what we should have done." Ice sat beside me on the couch and started to trace circles around my nipples with his fingertip. "We should all have masks that cover all of our faces. Then we could swap them and not know who was who. Of course, then my mouth would be covered." He leaned in to lick one of my stiff peaks.

"We could always put a blindfold on Kennedy," Ares suggested.

"Definitely," Mannix agreed. "But not today. If she wants to see us like this, then that's how it will be." He grabbed my knees and yanked me forward until I flopped down onto my back.

Ares grabbed my feet and held them up to make it easier for Mannix to pull off my shorts and panties. Smiling under the purple mask, he bent my knees and spread my legs wide, opening me out for them all to see.

"Shame your mouth is covered," he said to

Mannix. He all but shoved him aside and dove his face down between my legs.

Mannix grunted and undid his jeans before he grabbed the back of Ice's head and guided him to his already erect cock.

Ice eagerly opened his mouth and let Mannix slide his cock between his lips.

Fuck, that was hot every time.

I grabbed one of Ice's thighs and pulled him over closer. I turned my head and put my own mouth on his cock. He responded with I sounded like a pleased grunt and twisted a little further so I could take him in deeper.

The same time, Ares teased my clit with his tongue, sometimes using only slight pressure, some-times using a lot. Apparently he was inspired by Mannix edging me the other night. Pussy tease.

Instead of arguing or getting frustrated, I focused on sucking and licking, and tracing lines and circles around Ice's magic cross while Ares pushed me closer to the edge, then pulled me back again a handful of times.

Finally, he licked with more persistence. He slipped his fingers inside me and hooked them around to work me inside and out.

"Come for us," Mannix said. He was the only one

who didn't have his mouth full. Maybe having it covered wasn't so bad after all, he could boss us around.

I hung on to Ice's cock with one hand while I took my mouth off him and came. I arched my back, lifting up off the couch. My face tilted back, I shouted toward the ceiling.

Ice grunted in response. His cock throbbed in my fingers before he came, spilling himself down my cheek and chest. Strings of pearly cum decorated my skin and hair.

"Fuck, yeah," Mannix said breathlessly. "You look even more beautiful like that."

I smiled back at him.

Ares knelt in front of me and gripped my hips to pull me onto his thick, rock hard cock.

I groaned unashamedly. "You feel so good."

"So do you." He gave me a minute or two to get used to him, then started to thrust rapidly, but evenly.

I watched him. I watched all three of them. One fucking me, one having his mouth fucked, one with the only part of him visible, his eyes, closed.

Yeah, those masks definitely weren't scary anymore.

"Touch yourself," Ares said.

Without hesitation, I placed my hands down between us and found my clit. With two, slow fingers I started to circle and rub myself.

Mannix pulled out of Ice's mouth, and turned him around until he was bent over the couch beside me. He grabbed a tube of lube up off the coffee table and squirted out a finger full. He rubbed his fingers over Ice's rear hole and tossed the tube aside, before positioning himself behind the other guy. He gripped Ice's hips and drove himself slowly inside.

"Fuck, that feels amazing," Ice said. "So full."

"So tight," Mannix grunted.

Holy shit, that was also hot.

Ares leaned forward to nip and bite my nipples, hard enough to hurt and leave marks. Just how I liked it.

I couldn't keep myself from coming again, stimulated by my touch and the thrusting of his cock. I locked my eyes on Mannix's as the stars exploded around me. I think I shouted, but I didn't know. All I knew was the incredible sensation and the way he came from watching me. His hips rolled, pushing him deeper, harder, quicker into Ice's ass.

Ice ground himself back against Mannix, drawing out his orgasm even longer.

"Fuck, yeah," Mannix managed to say. It sounded as though his teeth were clenched behind his mask.

Ares followed right behind, pounding into me, his whole body leaned over me as he came.

It wasn't until we all slumped down that Mannix slipped his mask back off his face and tossed it onto the coffee table.

Ice followed suit a moment later. "I don't know what I prefer to do with a mask on, kill or fuck. It might be a tie."

"Both at the same time?" Ares said as he pulled off his own mask.

Ice sighed exaggeratedly. "Now that would be living the dream. We should do that sometime."

"Whatever you want, babe," Mannix said as he pulled his cock out of Ice's ass.

"Yes." Ice grinned. "You guys are the best. The best family an Iceman ever had."

"The best family I ever had too," Ares agreed. He sat up a little, content to leave his cock inside me for a while longer.

"Yeah, you guys are all much better than the alternative," Mannix said dryly.

Ice patted his cheek. "You did the right thing, killing Leo. He couldn't get away with doing the things he did. Especially touching Kennedy." That seemed to be the worst part of it in their books.

Personally, I thought everything he did added up, but it was too late to argue anyway.

All I could do was smile and say, "I'm a lucky girl to have you guys. I don't know what I'd do without any of you."

"You never have to find out," Ares said softly. "You'd have to kill us all to get rid of us."

"In that case, I guess we're stuck with each other forever." That sounded perfect to me.

EPILOGUE
KENNEDY

"I'm glad you got through it all okay." Samuel Bell sipped his espresso. It didn't surprise me that he drank it black and unsweetened. He seemed to like living on the edge. That must be a mobster thing.

"I take it my assumptions about Leo were correct?"

I sipped my own coffee and looked across the table to him. "All of it," I agreed.

"It doesn't mean we're friends," Mannix told him. He sat between me and Bell on one side. Ares and Ice sat on the other.

"But it doesn't mean we can't be friends in the future," I said, giving Mannix a meaningful look.

He shrugged. "Maybe. We'll see."

"Old habits are difficult to break," Bell said.

"Especially when you spend your whole life learning them." He was clearly talking about himself as well.

"I guess it takes someone who hasn't been indoctrinated to see both sides," I said.

"As long as they don't let themselves be led in the wrong direction." Bell raised an eyebrow at Mannix.

"Or the right direction," Mannix said. He matched Bell's expression.

Bell rolled his eyes, but a smile tugged at the corners of his mouth. "Whatever you say. Do me one favour though. If you ever come after me again, please stay the hell off my desk."

He sipped while my face burned. Of course he had cameras in his office.

Awkward.

"I've explained to Chloe and Lila that you've surrendered all claim to the leadership of the Bell family," Bell said, potentially steering the conversation in a less embarrassing direction. "That doesn't mean you're excluded from my will."

"She doesn't need your money," Mannix snapped.

"Probably not, but she's still my daughter," Bell said, unruffled. "She'll get her share. Not that I intend to die anytime soon." He put down his cup on the smooth, timber surface of the coffee shop's table.

We'd agreed any get-togethers we had should take place in public, so no one could accuse us of conspiring against the Brantleys.

"However, I've given my other daughters the task of earning their place as the head of the family. Chloe is older, but Lila is more ruthless."

"How are they going to earn that place?" I asked carefully.

"They'll earn it at Brutham Academy," he said. "First year is the way the Academy differentiates between those who are worthy and those who aren't."

I frowned. "Wait, isn't that how a bunch of students die?"

"It is," Bell agreed.

I gaped at him, but Mannix actually looked impressed.

"Whichever twin survives gets to lead the family," he said. "They may both survive, but this year should clearly indicate which of them is strong enough to step into my shoes." Bell looked as though he didn't find anything even slightly wrong with any of this.

"What if one of them comes to me for help?" I asked.

"There are no rules," Bell said bluntly. "If they come to you and you choose to help them, that's your call. If you choose not to help them, that's also up to you."

Well, shit. That wasn't even the most fucked up thing I'd heard since I'd come to Dusk Bay, but it was pretty fucked up. I was almost starting to like my father, but I was very grateful I hadn't grown up in his world. I was even more grateful I'd already surrendered any claim to the leadership of the Bells. I had a feeling if I hadn't, this battle, or tournament, or whatever you want to call it, would include me too.

Hard pass.

"Wow," Ice said softly. "Let the games begin."

THANK YOU FOR READING! The games begin in Heartless. In the meantime, grab a bonus scene with Kennedy and her guys in Ice's workroom here.

If you like steamy fantasy, Song of Blood and Binding is up next!

ABOUT THE AUTHOR

Maggie Alabaster writes reverse harem and, paranormal, sci-fi and fantasy romance.

She lives in NSW, Australia with one spouse, two daughters, one dog, and countless birds.

Jo Bradley writes contemporary romance.

Sign up for Maggie's newsletter! Sign Up!

Join Maggie's reader group! Join here!

Follow Maggie on Bookbub! Click here to follow me!

Check out Maggie's website- www. maggiealabaster.com

Novella Venomous

Saving Abbie books 1-4

Saving Abbie books 4-6 + Venomous

Ruthless Claws

Book 1 Ivory

Book 2 Crimson

Book 3 Elodie

Harmony's Magic

Book 1 Summoned by Fire

Book 2 Summoned by Fate

Book 3 Summoned by Desire

Shifter's Vault

Book 1 Discarded

Book 2 Deceived

Book 3 Disgraced

My Alien Mates

Book 1 Star Warriors

Book 2 Star Defenders

Book 3 Star Protectors

Academy of Modern Magic

Book 1 Digital Magic

Book 2 Virtual Magic

Book 3 Logical Magic

Complete Collection

Summer's Harem

Book 1: Shimmer

Book 2: Glimmer

Book 3: Flicker

Complete collection

Short reads

Taken by the Snowmen

Jingle All the Way

Also by Maggie Alabaster and Erin Yoshikawa

Caught by the Tide

Book 1 –Pursued by Shadows

Book 2 Pursued by Darkness

Book 3 Pursued by Monsters